The Screech Owls' Northern Adventure

Roy MacGregor

McClelland & Stewart

An M&S Paperback Original from
McClelland & Stewart Ltd.

Library and Archives Canada Cataloguing in Publication

MacGregor, Roy, 1948–
    The Screech Owls' northern adventure

(The Screech Owls series)
"An M&S paperback original."
ISBN 978-0-7710-5628-4

I. Title. II. Series: MacGregor, Roy, 1948– .
The Screech Owls series.

PS8575.G84S37 1996 jC813'.54 C96-930512-5
PZ7.M33SC 1996

We acknowledge the financial support of the Government of
Canada through the Book Publishing Industry Development
Program for our publishing activities. We further acknowledge
the support of the Canada Council for the Arts and the Ontario
Arts Council for our publishing program.

Cover illustration by Gregory C. Banning
Typeset in Bembo by M&S, Toronto

Printed and bound in the United States of America

McClelland & Stewart Ltd.
75 Sherbourne Street
Toronto, Ontario
M5A 2P9
www.mcclelland.com

8 9 10 11 12 14 13 12 11 10

for Trevor, Tarek, David, Lyle, Stan, Steve, Gord, Justin . . .

ACKNOWLEDGEMENTS

The author is grateful to Doug Gibson, who thought up this series, and to Alex Schultz, who pulls it off. He is also indebted to the people of Waskaganish, James Bay, for their hospitality. Thanks in particular to the wonderful Diamond family.

"I'M GONNA HURL!"

Five rows away, Travis Lindsay could hear Nish moaning into a pillow. He could hear him over the tinny pound of the Walkman hanging loosely off Data's bent ears as he dozed in the next seat. He could hear him over the clatter of the serving cart and the shouting coming from Derek and Dmitri as they played a game of hearts in the row behind. He could even hear Nish over the unbelievable roar of the engines.

How could anyone sleep at a time like this? Travis wondered, glancing at Data. This was the first time Travis had flown, and it hadn't been at all what he had imagined. This was no ten-minute helicopter lift at the fall fair; nor was it like the big, smooth passenger jet his father took once a month to business meetings in Montreal. This was three solid hours of howling engines, air pockets, and broken cloud. They were headed, it seemed, for the North Pole. They had all driven to Val d'Or, Quebec, the day before, and from there it was 1,500 kilometres further north by air to their final destination: Waskaganish, a native village on the shore of James Bay.

They were on a Dash 8, an aircraft that Data – who knew everything about computers and National Hockey League statistics, but nothing whatsoever about life – claimed could take off and land in the palm of your hand. This was an exaggeration, of course, but Travis had felt it wasn't far off when the cramped fifty-seat plane taxied out onto the runway, revved the engines hard once, and seemed to shoot straight off the ground into the low clouds.

Travis had barely taken a second breath by the time the plane rose through the clouds and into the sunshine hidden beyond. It was as if the cabin of the plane were being painted with melted gold. Blinded by the sudden light, Data lowered the window-shade, but Travis had reached across and raised it again. He wanted to see everything.

The pilot had come on the intercom and warned them that the flight might be bumpy and that he'd be leaving the seatbelt sign on. The flight attendant would have to wait before bringing out the breakfast cart.

The coaches and several parents, Travis's included, were sitting toward the back of the plane. Data's and Wilson's and Fahd's parents were all there. Perhaps they wanted to make sure nothing went wrong this time the way it had in Toronto.

The three boys hadn't missed a game or

practice since Muck let them come back at the end of a month-long suspension over the unfortunate shoplifting incident at the Hockey Hall of Fame. They'd apologized to the team and they'd missed a key tournament, and eventually Muck figured they'd learned their lesson. Travis knew they had. He'd talked to Data on the telephone almost every night during his suspension, and he knew that several times Data had been in tears.

Jesse Highboy was sitting directly across from Travis. Beside him were his father and mother and his Aunt Theresa, the Chief of Waskaganish. No one called her Theresa or even Mrs. Ottereyes – they all called her "Chief." She had come down to Val d'Or to welcome the Screech Owls, and now she was bringing them all to Northern Quebec for the First Nations Pee Wee Hockey Tournament, which would feature, for the first time, a non-native peewee hockey team: the Screech Owls.

Jesse's father had set it up. He had met with the team and parents and talked to them about the chance of a lifetime. The hockey would be a part of the trip, he had stressed, but the real reward would come in getting to experience the North and the native culture. All they had to do was get there. The people of Waskaganish were so pleased with the idea that they'd offered to put everyone up, players and parents, free of charge. No wonder so many hands had gone up when Mr. Highboy asked for a show of interest.

The Owls had held bottle drives and organized car washes, and the parents had worked so many bingos that Mr. Lindsay celebrated the end of them by burying his smoke-filled "bingo clothes" in a deep hole behind the garage. The team had read up on the North and were excited about what they had learned: the northern lights, caribou, traplines, the midnight sun.

"It's *spring*, not summer!" Willie Granger, the team trivia expert, had pointed out to those Owls, like Nish, who figured they'd never have to go to bed and could stay up all night long. "Day and night are just about equal this time of year – same as where we live." But no one expected anything else to be the same. No one.

Perhaps, Travis wondered, this was why Nish had been acting so oddly. In the weeks leading up to the trip, Nish had kidded Jesse mercilessly.

"Should I bring a bow and arrow?" Nish had asked. "Will we be living in teepees?"

Some of it had been pretty funny, Travis had to admit, but it left him feeling a bit uneasy. Travis knew that the general rule of a hockey dressing room was "anything goes," and certainly Jesse had handled Nish's cracks easily, laughing and shooting back insults, but Travis still found it intriguing that no one other than Nish took such shots.

No one expected teepees. But beyond that they didn't really know what to expect.

Chief Ottereyes and Air Creebec, the airline

that set up the charter, had put on a special break-fast for the Owls. Once the turbulence had settled enough, the flight attendant handed out a breakfast the likes of which no Screech Owl, Jesse Highboy excepted, had ever seen. There were tiny things like tea biscuits that Chief Ottereyes explained were "bannock – just like we cook up out on the trapline." And there was fish, but not cooked like anything Travis had ever seen at a fish-and-chip shop. This fish was dry and broke apart easily. At first Travis wasn't too sure, but when he tasted it he thought it was more like *candy* than fish. "Smoked whitefish," Chief Ottereyes said. "Smoked and cured with sugar."

"I got no knife and fork!" Nish had shouted from his seat.

Chief Ottereyes laughed: "You've got hands, haven't you?"

"Yeah."

"Clamp 'em over your mouth, then!" Wilson had called from the other side of the plane.

"This is traditional Cree food!" Chief Ottereyes had leaned forward and told Nish.

"I'll take a traditional Egg McMuffin, thank you!" Nish called back.

He wouldn't try the food. Instead, he'd dug down into the carry-on bag he had stuffed beneath his seat and hauled out three chocolate bars and sat stuffing his face with one hand while he used the other to hold his nose as though he couldn't stand the smell of the smoked fish.

They had just been finishing up this unusual breakfast when the plane rattled as if it had just hit a pothole. The "fasten your seatbelt" light flashed and the pilot had come on the intercom to tell the attendant to stop picking up the trays and hang on, they were about the enter some more choppy air.

"I'M GONNA HURL!"

With the plane starting to buck, the attendant was unable to move forward to help Nish in case he was, in fact, going to be sick. Instead, she passed ahead a couple of Gravol air-sickness pills, a juice to wash them down, and a barf bag in case the worst happened. Nish took the pills and soon began moaning.

After a while, when the plane began to settle again, Nish called out, "Can I get a blanket?"

Travis thought Nish was acting like a baby. The attendant handed over a blanket, and the players behind Nish tossed theirs over, too. He wrapped himself tight and pressed his face into the pillow, then closed his eyes and continued to moan.

The pilot took the plane to a higher altitude, and the flight once again smoothed out. Derek and Dmitri's card game started up again, the attendant completed her collection of the breakfast trays, and Nish moaned on.

Data stood up in the aisle. "I think he needs a

few more blankets!" he called out, grinning mischievously. "I can still hear him."

Blankets and pillows by the dozen headed in Data's direction. Even Muck, shaking his head in mock disgust, handed his over. Data, now helped by Wilson, stacked them on poor Nish until he could be neither seen nor heard.

"There," Data announced. "That ought to hold him."

Nish never budged. Travis figured he must have gone to sleep. He hoped he was able to breathe all right through the blankets, but it was nice not to have to listen to him any longer. Travis turned toward the window and thought about the tournament and how he would play. He felt great these days. Hockey was a funny game: sometimes when you didn't feel well but played anyway, you had the most wonderful game; sometimes when you felt fantastic, you played terribly.

He tried to imagine himself playing in Waskaganish, but he couldn't. He couldn't picture the rink. He couldn't imagine the village. He could not, for the first time in his life, even imagine the players on the other side. Would they be good players? Rough? Smart? Would they have different rules up here? No, they couldn't have. He was getting tired, too tired to think . . .

". . . put your seats in the upright position, fasten your tables back, and ensure that all carry-on luggage is safely stowed under the seat in front of you. Thank you."

The announcement and the sudden sense that something was happening woke Travis with a start. He could hear seats being moved, tables being fastened, excitement rising.

"I can see the village!" Derek shouted from behind.

Travis leaned toward the window. He could see James Bay stretching away like an ocean, the ice along the shore giving way to water that was steel grey and then silver where the sun bounced on the waves.

The plane was beginning to rock again. The plane came down low over the water, then began to bank back toward the village. Travis could see a hundred or more houses. He could see a church, and a large yellow building like a huge machine shed. The rink? He could see the landing strip on the right: one long stretch of ploughed ground.

Just then, they hit a huge air pocket. The plane banked sharply and seemed to slide through the air sideways before righting itself with a second tremendous jolt.

"HELP MEEEEEEEE!!"

Travis could hear Nish screaming over the roar of the engines and the landing gear grinding down into position. No one could go to him. They were landing.

"I'M DYINNNGGG!" Nish screamed from beneath his blankets.

The big plane came down and hammered into the ground, bounced twice, and settled, the engines roaring as the pilot immediately began to brake. The howl was extraordinary.

Nish moaned and cried until the plane slowed and turned abruptly off the landing strip toward an overgrown shed that had a sign, WASKAGANISH, over the doorway. There was a big crowd gathered. It seemed the whole town was out to greet the Screech Owls.

"HELP MEEEE!!" Nish moaned. Travis had never heard such a pathetic sound.

Finally, as the plane came to a halt, the attendant got up and began pulling off Nish's blankets, digging him out, until his big, red-eyed face was blinking up at her in surprise.

"I thought we'd crashed," he said, "and I was the only survivor." Everyone on the plane broke up.

The attendant just shook her head. Travis couldn't tell if she was amused or disgusted.

"You wouldn't want to survive," the Chief told him. "You'd never make it out of the bush alive, my friend."

Nish looked up, blinking. "I *wouldn't*?"

"Of course not," she said, then reached over and pinched Nish's big cheek.

"The Trickster eats fat little boys like you!"

Nish looked blank. What *was* she talking about?

2

TRAVIS FELT THE DIFFERENCE AS SOON AS THE DOOR of the Dash 8 opened. It was like walking into a rink on a hot day in August. The unexpected cold was shocking. The Screech Owls had started the journey in spring-like weather, but it seemed now they had travelled all they way back into winter.

Quickly pulling on their team jackets, the Owls spilled out of the plane and down the steps, where they were met by a greeting party the likes of which none of them had ever imagined. People stood in the backs of pick-up trucks, banging their fists on the cab roofs while those inside the cabs honked their horns. Young men and women revved their snowmobile engines. Some two hundred villagers stood about in thick winter clothing, stomping their feet to keep warm and applauding, the laughter and shouts of the people of Waskaganish hanging above their heads in quick clouds of winter breath.

A gang of youngsters moved toward the Screech Owls. They had to be a hockey team, Travis figured; they wore matching jackets with an animal face on it. But it was an animal he had never seen before. It looked a bit like a bear, a bit like a wolf, a bit like a skunk. The letters underneath the face (if they even were letters) meant nothing to him.

Giggling, the Cree team moved to one side to reveal one shorter player carrying a huge boom box. He hit a button and the air filled with the pounding lyrics of the rock group Queen:

> *We will,*
> *We will,*
> *ROCK YOU!*

Everyone laughed – everyone but the Screech Owls, who didn't know what to make of this. It seemed a great joke to all the locals, including Chief Ottereyes, who made her way to the front of the gathering and held up her right hand. Instantly, the boom box was switched off.

"What I'd give for that kind of authority," Muck muttered just behind Travis. He could hear some of the parents laughing, but they obviously didn't know Muck, Travis thought. When Muck had a certain look in his eyes, he didn't even need to raise his hand to bring the Screech Owls' dressing room to full attention.

The Chief turned to address the Screech Owls. She seemed to be smiling right at Travis.

"The people of Waskaganish welcome the

Screech Owls to our village. Please consider our home your home for the next five days."

The villagers applauded in agreement. Even the team was clapping, Travis noticed. Perhaps they weren't so bad, after all.

The Chief then spoke in Cree. It was a language Travis had never heard before, and every so often the villagers laughed as if it were some great inside joke.

Nish, too, was laughing.

"What's she saying, Data?" he whispered.

"How the heck would I know?"

"You're the only one on the team who speaks Klingon, aren't you?"

Chief Ottereyes returned to English. "Could we have the Screech Owls' captains come forward, please?"

Travis felt a slight nudge at his back. It was Muck, gently encouraging. Travis stepped forward and signalled for his assistant captains, Derek and Nish, to follow him. Nish seemed extremely reluctant, shaking his head and giggling nervously as he pushed through the protection of the Screech Owls crowd.

"And the captains of the Wolverines . . . ?" the Chief added.

Wolverines? Was *that* the animal on their jackets? Travis had never seen a wolverine.

A lanky young man shrugged and moved forward. On the arm of his jacket was the number 7, the same number Travis wore. On the other arm the name "Jimmy" was stitched.

Behind the Wolverines' captain came the three assistants. Travis studied them quickly. One, a big, thick kid with a bit of a scowl. The second, a skinny kid with a Toronto Maple Leafs cap on backwards, and, underneath the cap, fur earmuffs. And the third . . . a *girl!* Travis hadn't noticed her. He was surprised, but he knew he shouldn't be. The Screech Owls' previous captain had been Sarah Cuthbertson, and she had been their best player. And they'd had Sareena in goal back then, and now they had Liz and Chantal and Jennie. But still, he hadn't expected to find a girl on a team up here in the North. He thought it would be more like when his dad played and his mother had never even learned how to hold a hockey stick. He didn't know why he thought it would be that way here. He just did.

"Travis Lindsay and Jimmy Whiskeyjack are the two team captains," Chief Ottereyes announced. "And Jimmy has a gift for Travis."

Travis didn't know how to react. A gift? He hadn't brought anything to give in return.

Jimmy Whiskeyjack reached inside his pocket, withdrew a small flat blue box, and handed it to Travis. Travis took it, and then took Jimmy's free hand, which was also extended. Travis shook, wondering if his grip was strong enough.

Travis looked up at Chief Ottereyes. She was

smiling encouragement. "Go ahead," she said. "Open it up so we can all see."

Travis knew everyone was looking at him. He lifted the lid and stared at the object inside. He hadn't a clue what it was: a twig tied in a circle containing a loose web of string, and feathers tied to the side.

He looked up at the Chief. "Go ahead, Travis. Take it out," she told him.

Travis removed the strange object and held it up. Some of the Screech Owls' parents *oooh*ed and *ahhh*ed. It was beautiful. The sun danced in the colours of the feathers.

"It's a dream catcher," Jimmy Whiskeyjack said.

Chief Ottereyes explained. "It's an Ojibway dream catcher. There's an old legend that says one of these will catch all your dreams. The good ones pass through into your future. The bad ones are caught, and when the sun comes out in the morning, it destroys them."

"*Looks like a goldfish net,*" Nish hissed to Derek. Travis heard, and hoped no one else did. He wished Nish was still buried in blankets.

"It was made by Rachel Highboy," the Chief announced, "the Wolverines' assistant captain."

Everyone applauded the slim girl who had stepped out with Jimmy Whiskeyjack. She blushed and looked at Travis, who was still holding up the dream catcher for all to see. Travis felt funny inside. The effects of the plane ride maybe. He hoped he wouldn't have to say anything.

He didn't. On a cue from Chief Ottereyes, Jimmy Whiskeyjack stepped forward and shook Travis's hand again. Jimmy then stepped past him and shook hands with Derek and Nish. The other assistants from the Wolverines came to shake hands as well.

Travis took Rachel Highboy's hand and was surprised by how small it felt in his. No way could she be a player, Travis thought. She held on.

Travis looked up. She had large dark eyes and her long black hair was whipping in the wind. She smiled, and Travis felt like he was still in the plane, with the bottom dropping out of it.

3

TRAVIS HAD HEARD ABOUT GETTING YOUR SEA LEGS
– when you could finally stand on the deck of a
ship and roll with the waves instead of hanging
weak-kneed and sick over the railing – but after
the plane ride he had to wonder if Nish was
having trouble getting back his *land* legs.

They had been on the ground for more than
three hours, but Nish was still wobbly. That was
fine when they had just been getting set up with
their billets – Travis and Nish were placed with
the Wolverines' captain, Jimmy Whiskeyjack, and
his family – but it was quite another matter now
that they were all out on the ice, about to play
their first game of the First Nations Pee Wee
Hockey Tournament.

The Screech Owls had drawn the Moose
Factory Mighty Geese as their first opponents.
The Owls would have an easy time of it, Jimmy
had predicted as he helped Travis carry his equipment over to the rink. The Mighty Geese didn't
have much of a team; they didn't even have a
proper rink to practice or play in. Instead they
played outside, and the last time the Wolverines

had gone to Moose Factory, they had been forced to cancel the third period on account of the wind. It was knocking players over.

None of the teams over on the Ontario side of James Bay were all that good, Jimmy continued. They were all Cree, but the Ontario Cree were very poor and didn't have much to spend on hockey. The Quebec Cree were better off. It was on the Quebec side, through land owned by the Quebec Cree and Inuit, that the big rivers flowed into James Bay and where the huge hydro-electric dams had been built. They had opposed the projects, he explained, but when they realized they couldn't stop them, they made a deal with the governments that had given them things like airstrips and new houses and a school and a brand-new hockey rink. They had *two* Zambonis, just like Maple Leaf Gardens!

"If one breaks down," Jimmy had explained, "you can't just drive a new one in through the bush."

The ice was terrific. As usual, Travis let the Owls' two goaltenders – Jenny Staples and Jeremy Weathers – lead the team out onto the ice, but he made sure he was next. And while Jenny and Jeremy both skated straight to the near net to place their water bottles, Travis burst for centre ice, his head down so he could see the marks his skates left as they dug in deep. Good old Mr. Dillinger: another perfect sharpening job, with the blades sharp enough that when he cornered on new ice they made a sound like bacon frying.

The other Screech Owls came out behind him. Dmitri Yakushev, the Owls' best skater, dug down deep and flew around the new ice. Derek, Gordie, Data, big Andy Higgins, Liz, who was fast becoming one of the team's smoothest skaters, Lars – all leaned deep into their turns to produce that sweet clean cut and spray that is possible only on fresh-flooded ice.

After looking around at the others, Travis found Nish, flat on his back in the Owls' far corner. He dug in and raced around, stopping in a one-skate spray.

Nish just lay there, staring straight up.

"What the heck are you doing?" Travis asked.

Nish blinked once. "*Stretching*," he said.

Out by the red line at centre ice, Travis began his own stretches, alone and quiet, the way he liked it. While he stretched, he studied the Moose Factory team. Their sweaters were all right, with a laughing goose on the front that looked a bit like Daffy Duck. But no matching socks. And the equipment! Travis had never seen a team so poorly outfitted. The Mighty Geese were lined up at the blueline to take shots, and two of the players were sharing a stick, one of them waiting until the other had shot and then throwing the stick to him when he raced back.

The referee called for the two captains, and Travis skated over. When the captain of the Mighty Geese joined him, Travis saw he was one of the players who had been sharing the stick.

"Shake hands, boys," the referee said. "Let's have a good, clean game, okay?"

The Mighty Geese captain stared as Travis slapped his stick, not his hand, into his opponent's outstretched palm.

Travis had done it without even thinking. He had brought three sticks with him, all brand new, but he didn't need all three.

"You're short a stick," Travis said. "Take this. I brought extras."

The other captain stared at it, tried it once (he shot left, the same as Travis), then nodded. He took Travis's hand and shook hard.

"Thanks a lot."

"Just don't score too many goals," Travis said, and grinned.

The captain smiled back. He had two broken front teeth. Travis wanted to ask what had happened. Was it a puck? A stick? Not likely — everyone here wore a full face-mask. It had to be from something other than hockey. A fall? . . . A fist?

Muck seemed concerned. Before the actual face-off, he called the Owls over for a quick huddle by the bench. He usually did this only when they had a big game, a championship, to decide, but this time he seemed every bit as serious.

"No fancy stuff, now," he said. "I want to see a team out there, not fifteen individual superstars."

By the end of his first shift, Travis knew exactly what Muck meant. The Screech Owls were badly outclassing the Mighty Geese. The Owls were better skaters, better positional players, better passers and shooters, and they had three good lines, whereas the Geese only had the one, centred by the captain with Travis's stick.

Nish couldn't resist. You put Nish on the ice against a weak lineup, and it was as if he'd had too much sugar on his cereal. Wobbly-legged or not, he couldn't help himself. He picked up the puck at the blueline and skated, *backwards*, into his own end and around the net past Jennie, who'd been given the first start. He then slipped it through the other captain's skates, and came hard down the ice, with Dmitri on one side charging fast.

Nish turned backwards as he reached the last Mighty Geese defenceman and attempted the "spinnerama," a move Nish claimed had come to him in a daydream during music class but which Willie Granger said had been used in the NHL by everyone from Bobby Orr to Denis Savard before Nish was even born.

It didn't matter to Nish. He believed he had invented it, and he had certainly invented this version of it. He spun directly in front of the defender, lost his footing, and crashed, butt first, into the backing-up defenceman. Both went down. Travis heard the scream of the poor defenceman as Nish's full weight landed on his chest and they slid in a pile past the puck, left sitting there for Travis as if it were glued to the ice.

Dmitri gave one quick rap on the ice with the heel of his stick and Travis cuffed the puck quickly across. Dmitri one-timed his shot into the open side of the Mighty Geese's net to the shriek of the referee's whistle.

First shift, 1–0 Screech Owls!

Travis threw his arms around Dmitri as Dmitri spun around behind the net, his arms raised in triumph. They smashed into the boards together and felt the crush of their teammates hitting them. Travis could hear, and feel, Nish, and there was no mistaking the whine in his voice.

"They better give me an assist on that one – I set it up!"

Travis could see the referee out of the corner of his eye, and he didn't like what he saw. The ref's arms were crossing back and forth down low, the sign of a goal being waved off. And now he was raising one hand and pointing with the other at the crush of Owls in the corner. The whistle blew again.

"*No goal?*" Travis called out. The scrum of players broke, all turning to look at the referee.

"*You're outta here, Number 4!*" the referee shouted as he closed in on the celebrating Screech Owls. "*Two minutes for interference!*"

"*What the h–?*"

The curse was barely out of Nish's mouth when up went the arm again, and again the whistle blew.

"*And two more for unsportsmanlike conduct!*"

Travis looked at Nish. His face was scrunched up like a game's worth of used shinpad tape, but at least his big mouth was shut.

Nish got into the penalty box, and the Mighty Geese went ahead when a shot from the point took a funny bounce off their captain's stick – the stick Travis had given to him – the puck dribbling in behind a flopping, scrambling Jennie.

Nish got out on the goal. He skated over as if he were dragging the Zamboni behind him, and never even lifted his head to see what Muck was thinking. He knew. He was in the doghouse. Without being told he moved down the bench and took a place on the very end.

Travis got a tap on the back of his shoulder and leapt over the boards onto the ice with Dmitri and Derek. They knew what to do. Travis won the face-off back to Data, Data clipped it off the boards to a breaking Dmitri – and Dmitri swept around the Mighty Geese defenceman so fast the defenceman fell straight backwards as his feet tangled. Dmitri went in and deked twice, sending the goaltender down and entirely out of the net, and then he roofed the puck so high he broke the goalie's water battle open. It was like a fountain bursting behind the empty net.

Wolverines 1, Screech Owls 1.

Next shift out for Travis, Dmitri's speed caught the Mighty Geese on a bad line change, and the Screech Owls went ahead to stay. They went on to win 5–2, and when the two teams shook hands at the end, the captain slammed his stick into Travis's shin pads, a salute of thanks for the stick. Travis couldn't help but note again that several Mighty Geese had no gloves on. They had to be sharing gloves. No wonder the Owls had caught them short on line changes.

Travis could hear the crowd applauding them as they skated off. He looked up and saw the Wolverines' assistant standing on a bench, clapping. *Rachel*. He yanked his helmet off, then began pushing his hair down. It was wet, and he worried that it was sticking up where it shouldn't be.

4

THAT NIGHT THERE WAS A BANQUET TO CELEBRATE the start of the First Nations Pee Wee Hockey Tournament. The Screech Owls, all in team jackets, white turtlenecks, and dark pants, were seated at one long table to the side. Muck, the assistant coaches, and Mr. Dillinger, the team manager, sat at the end nearest the head table, and Travis, Data, Jesse, and Nish were at the far end. But it still wasn't far enough away for Travis.

Nish had brought some of his candy stash with him, and laid it out on his plate: a Caramilk bar, a couple of green licorice twists, a Twinkie, a pair of Reese peanut-butter cups.

"A balanced diet," he announced as he laid it all out and pointed deliberately to the licorice. "Right down to my greens."

What had got into Nish?

Chief Ottereyes had announced that a traditional Cree feast would be held at the community hall. There were Cree drummers pounding as the eight teams playing in the tournament had entered: the Screech Owls, the Wolverines, the Mighty Geese, the Northern Lights, the Caribou, the Trappers, the Belugas, and the Maple Leafs. (Jesse Highboy had pointed out that there were no maple trees this far north, but they picked up the Toronto Maple Leaf broadcasts by satellite.) The Screech Owls were the only non-native team. The Mighty Geese were the only group without team jackets.

The banquet opened with a long Cree prayer recited by an elder, then Chief Ottereyes talked a bit about life along James Bay. It was a speech clearly meant for the visitors from the South. She talked about the history of the area, a history that white people like to date from 1611, when the British explorer Henry Hudson sailed into this bay and anchored at the mouth of the Rupert River, "which you can see for yourself if you just step outside the front door here," she added. The Crees, however, preferred to say that 1611 was the year they discovered the white man.

The Chief told them the Crees had had to learn to accept other languages and other religions and customs, and that the visitors should feel free to ask any questions they might have about how the Cree lived in the North. "Tonight," she said, "you will be eating traditional Cree food. This is the diet we have lived on for centuries – and we're still here, so enjoy."

She sat down to great applause, no one clapping louder than the Screech Owls. They began serving the meal immediately, starting with bannock. Nish, however, would have nothing to do with it.

"You can't eat just junk," Travis warned.

"You'll make yourself sick again," Jesse added.

"I'll make myself sick if I have to watch you people eat," Nish snapped back.

The feast proceeded: huge bowls of boiled potatoes, moose stew, caribou steaks, cheese, smoked whitefish, fried trout. At one point, a large bowl was carried past the Screech Owls that seemed, at first glance, to have a small hand sticking up from it.

"GROSS!" Nish shouted before Travis could even point it out to Jesse.

"*What is it?*" Travis hissed at Jesse.

Jesse Highboy was laughing. He stood up and excused himself as he picked up the bowl from the next table. Inside was, indeed, a small hand sticking up. An arm and a wrist and a . . . *paw*.

"Beaver," Jesse said, matter-of-factly.

"BEAVER?" Nish howled. "WHAT'S NEXT . . . SKUNK?"

Travis cringed. People were staring. Some were laughing at Nish. Some, like Rachel Highboy, were definitely not impressed.

Jesse handled it perfectly. "Beaver is a very special food here," he said.

"I thought you trapped beaver for fur," Data said.

"We do. But even if no one in the world wore

26

fur coats, we'd still trap beaver. It's our food up here, same as cattle and chickens are your food down south. You think the original natives went after beaver so they could wear fancy fur coats?"

Data had clearly never thought about this. Neither had Travis. He had presumed trapping was wrong because it hurt. But as Jesse had once said, did he think that cows and chickens *volunteered* for McDonald's?

"I'm gonna hurl!" Nish said, opening up his Caramilk and laughing a bit too loudly. Travis glanced down the table. He could see Muck was watching. He did not look happy.

Jesse tried another approach. "Look, Nish, do you like crackle?

"Crackle?"

"Yeah, you know, the hard outside when your mom cooks a pork roast."

"Oh, that. Yeah, you bet, I *love* it!"

Jesse signalled to a woman who was carrying a tray to the head table. She stopped and smiled as Jesse stood, checked the tray, then helped himself to a plate piled high with what seemed like slices of bacon that were all fat and no meat.

Jesse took a fork and placed a slice carefully on Nish's plate right beside the licorice twists – Nish's *greens*. He stood back: "See what you think of ours."

Nish sniffed, then nodded happily. "*This* I can relate to," he said.

He picked up his knife and fork, cut a piece off, placed it in his mouth, and chewed happily.

"First rate," Nish pronounced. "My compliments to the chef."

"What about to the hunter?" Jesse asked.

Nish opened his eyes, blinking. "You *hunt* pigs up here?"

"Who said it was pig?"

"You did – pork crackle."

"Call it crackle if you like," Jesse said, "but it isn't pork."

Nish stopped chewing. "What is it then?"

Jesse turned to the woman carrying the tray. "Tell him," he said. "He won't believe me."

The woman smiled at Nish. "Moose nostrils," she said. "Would you like some more?"

Nish looked as if he was about to pass out.

"*I'm gonna hurl*," he repeated, spitting his food out onto his plate.

Muck had seen enough. He got up and walked straight down the aisle toward Nish, who winced when he saw him coming.

"Outta here, Nishikawa," Muck ordered.

There could be no fooling. When Muck used that tone, you jumped. When Muck used last names, you jumped twice as fast. Nish scrambled to his feet and, with Muck at his elbow, was escorted out of the banquet room.

TRAVIS HAD NEVER SEEN NISH SO QUIET. THEY HAD all returned to their billets, and the Whiskeyjacks had put out hot chocolate and cookies for the boys, but Nish was hardly even sipping his.

Travis had no idea what Muck had said to Nish, but he knew Muck wouldn't have minced his words. Nish was clearly out of sorts. As they'd washed up in the bathroom, he'd told Travis he wished he'd never come. "If there was a road outta here," he said, "I'd hitchhike."

"You haven't even given it a chance," Travis said.

"It sucks."

"It's just different."

"Gimme a break. No movie theatres, no McDonald's, no corner stores, no buses, no cable TV, no video arcade, not even a pathetic T-shirt for me to buy."

"There's more to going different places than getting a T-shirt."

Nish made a big face. "This is *backwards*, man. Open your eyes. We're in the Stone Age here – the Ice Age by the feel of it."

There was no point in arguing. They went out

and sat with Jimmy Whiskeyjack and his big family – father, mother, grandmother, two sisters, and three younger brothers – and drank hot chocolate and talked while Nish kept looking at the TV in the corner as if he wished he could turn it on just by staring at it.

Normally, that's what Travis would have been doing, too, but the Whiskeyjacks showed no inclination whatsoever to turn to the TV. Instead of sitting in a half circle around it, they sat in a full circle around the kitchen table. The younger kids played and listened, and Travis and Jimmy – but not Nish – talked a bit about the hockey tournament. Most of the talk, however, came from the grandmother, translated either by Jimmy's mother or father.

In this house, the grandmother was like the TV. They all stared at her and listened as if she were some special program they'd been allowed to stay up and watch.

It was fascinating. She and her husband had both trapped, and six of her nine children had been born in the bush, as she had been before them. Through her daughter, Jimmy's mother, she told how two of them had died and how they had buried the babies in the bush and marked the graves, and how they would go back to visit them every year, right up until 1979.

The old woman took a long, long pause. Travis couldn't help but ask: "Why 1979?"

Jimmy's mother answered. There were tears in her eyes. "That's when they flooded my parents' trapline."

"Flooded?"

"The dams," Jimmy explained. "The hydro dams. The graves are under sixty feet of water."

"Didn't anybody tell them there were graves there?"

Travis's question made Jimmy's parents laugh. They translated this to the grandmother, and she shook her head angrily.

"We tried," explained Jimmy's father. "But they didn't even tell us they were going to do it."

The old woman clearly did not want to dwell on this part of her story. She launched into a tale that soon had everyone laughing again, but as Jimmy's father translated, Travis realized it was really about her family almost starving to death.

The grandmother told how, one year, the beaver had all but vanished from their trapline, and her husband had left her alone with the children while he followed the trail of the caribou herd, hoping to return with food before the little they had left ran out.

He did not come back in time. The food was just about gone. Christmas was coming and she had nothing to give the children – usually she would have bought some sweets at the Hudson's Bay store and hidden them until Christmas Day.

Christmas Eve it had snowed. And when they

woke the next morning, the sun was bright and the new snow sparkled like white gold, so bright they had to squint when they turned back the flap of the tent. The old woman told her children that it had snowed sugar during the night: a Christmas present for them. She made them line up at the doorway, and then she took a spoon, went out into the snow, and very carefully scooped some up. She brought it back and told the oldest child to close his eyes. He did, and when she gave him his present he licked his lips, saying it was the most delicious snow he had ever tasted. She then did the same thing for each of the younger ones, who were already waiting with mouths open and eyes closed.

"It really tasted just like sugar," said Jimmy's mother. "I can still taste it today."

Later in the day her husband returned with his sled piled high with caribou meat. They would make it through the winter. And none of them would ever forget the Christmas it snowed sugar in the bush.

Travis had never heard such a wonderful story. He was fighting back tears. His throat hurt. He looked at Nish, who was still staring longingly at the TV set as if he wished he were someplace else.

They talked a while, and Nish surprised Travis by suddenly turning and asking a question.

"What's a Trickster?"

Jimmy's mother looked at him, surprised. She glanced at her husband, then back at Nish.

"Where did you hear about the Trickster?"

"The Chief," Nish said. "She said if I got lost in the bush up here it would eat me."

Jimmy's parents laughed. The old woman fiercely worked her jaw.

"It's just an old story," Jimmy's mother said. "Like a fairytale."

The old woman said something sharp. Everyone turned to listen, even Travis and Nish, who couldn't understand a word.

Finally, Jimmy's mother explained. "My mother says the Trickster is real, no matter whether you can actually touch it or just feel it in your head. She says her own father said he saw it, that the Trickster came and punished a family that was being too selfish one winter and wouldn't share a caribou they had killed."

"What happened?" asked Jimmy.

His mother answered, but she didn't seem to believe. "The Trickster came and killed them and ate them."

"The Trickster is legend," Jimmy's father explained to Travis and Nish. "Many tribes have it in their myths. It's a monster that comes at night and either eats its victims or drives them insane. Myself, I think it probably grew out of tough times, people actually going mad in the bush and needing something to blame it on. People getting attacked by bears maybe and someone saying it was cannibalism."

Again the grandmother said something sharp. Jimmy's father answered her in an apologetic tone. Then he addressed the boys: "She says Cree hunters don't make things up."

"What's it look like?" Nish asked.

"No one knows," said Jimmy's mother. "There are lots of drawings, of course. Sometimes a monster with three heads. Sometimes with just one. But always with a head like a wolf and eyes like hot coals in a fire."

Jimmy's father checked his watch. "It's eleven o'clock, boys. We stay up all night, you'll be in no shape for your game tomorrow. Let's get to bed."

Travis and Nish were in bunk beds in Jimmy's room down in the basement. The three of them lay awake for a long time, talking quietly.

"You ever see this thing?" Nish asked.

"Of course not," answered Jimmy. "They used to warn us that he'd come and take us away if we weren't good."

"Like the bogeyman," said Travis.

"I guess," said Jimmy.

"Sounds stupid to me," said Nish. Then, after a long pause, he thought to add: "Sorry, Jimmy."

"Sounds stupid to me, too," Jimmy said. But he didn't sound particularly convincing.

6

THEY WERE AWAKENED AT DAWN THE NEXT MORN-
ing by Jimmy Whiskeyjack's father shouting
down at them from the top of the stairs. They had
an eight o'clock game against the Belugas, a team
from a community called Great Whale, another
hour north by air. But he wasn't calling to get
them up for the game.

"Come and see the geese!" he shouted.
"They're back!"

Jimmy kicked off his covers and was dressed in
an instant, already scrambling up the stairs as
Travis and Nish stood in their underwear trying
to rub the sleep out of their eyes.

"Didn't we just play them?" Nish asked in a
sleepy voice.

"That was the Mighty Geese," Travis said.
"These are *real* geese."

"You expect me to run outside to see a stupid
goose?"

"You can do whatever you want," Travis told
him. He was tired of putting up with his friend's
complaining. "I'm going out with Jimmy."

Travis bolted up the stairs and out the front

door, which had been left wide open as the entire family came out to see what all the fuss was about. Travis couldn't believe his ears: the honking sounded like something between a traffic jam and a schoolyard at recess.

The sky was filled with geese. There must have been half a dozen different V formations. One had only five geese in it, another, much higher, must have had two hundred. And the noise wasn't coming just from the sky; almost everyone standing in the roadways held their fists up to their mouths, honking back at the geese as if to say hello.

Travis went and stood by Jimmy, who kept pointing to new formations coming in from the south. "The spring goose-hunt is on now," he said. "Our hockey tournament just lost half its spectators."

"How come they all come at once?" Travis asked.

Jimmy laughed. "They don't. This is just the start. They'll be flying in for the next three weeks. It'll look like this every morning – some mornings there'll be twice this many. Aren't they beautiful?"

Travis agreed that they were. He had never seen such grace. He loved the way they seemed to be barely moving their wings. He loved the perfect distance they kept from each other, and the arrow–straight wedge they formed as they flew, the one in front sometimes dropping back so another could take the lead.

He looked back toward the house. Nish had come out and was standing on the porch steps, blinking as he looked up. He was shaking his head. He didn't seem impressed.

The Belugas were already on the ice when the Screech Owls skated out. Travis bolted past the goalies and made a wide circle at centre ice, pretending not even to notice the other team. He would have preferred to be out first, to be first on the fresh ice, but it was still clean and he could feel – and, even better, *hear* – his skates dig in with a perfect sharp. Dmitri and Derek had caught up to him and the three of them, in perfect unison, swept behind the net and came out in a perfect V as they headed fast down the ice, their strides smooth and evenly matched, their speed constant.

Just like the geese, Travis thought. He wondered if anyone else was thinking the same thing. Certainly not Nish, who was stretching by the boards. Nish had a look that said he was thinking only about hockey. Muck had plainly got to him.

They lined up for the face-off, and, for the first time, Travis took his measure of the opposition. The Great Whale team had beautiful sweaters, with an Inuit drawing of a big, white beluga whale on the front. And they were laughing, something Travis had never seen a team do before the puck dropped. They were speaking in Cree and pointing at Nish.

"Hey," one of them called in English, "*Moose Nostrils!*"

Travis turned quickly and glanced at his friend on the blueline. If Nish had heard, he was giving no indication of it. He looked as if the Stanley Cup final was about to begin.

The puck dropped, and Travis swept it back to Nish, who skated all the way back to his own end. Oh no, Travis thought, he's going to try to go coast-to-coast. Nish the Superstar.

But nothing of the sort. Nish deftly got one of the Belugas' wingers to race at him and left him behind the net as he burst out the other side. He hit Data with a perfect pass and Data played the give-and-go, feeding Nish the puck back at the blueline. Nish hit Derek at the red line, and Derek put a beautiful pass to Dmitri just as he hit the Belugas' blueline. Dmitri cut to the centre, dropped the puck, and took out his checker with a shoulder brush, leaving Travis to walk in alone, pull the goaltender down, and then send the puck back to Derek, who had the wide-open net to score in. *Tic-tac-tic-tac-toe.*

They lined up as the goal was announced:

"Derek Dillinger from Travis Lindsay and Dmitri Yakushev." Not even a mention of Nish's name, but everyone knew who had set up the play in the first place, including the Belugas.

"Hey, Moose Nostrils!" they called at him. "You hungry, Moose Nostrils?"

But Nish paid no attention. He was dead serious. He had come to play.

And a good thing too, for the Belugas were a good team, fast and tough, but lacking a strong third line like the Screech Owls'. Andy Higgins and Chantal Larochelle both scored, Lars (Cherry) Johanssen scored from the blueline on a screen, and the glove hand of Jeremy Weathers simply proved too fast for the Belugas' snipers.

The Screech Owls won easily, 4–1, and lined up quickly to shake hands with this excellent team. Nish was first in line, ready for what was coming as the other team filed by:

"Good game, Moose Nostrils!"

"Thank you very much."

"Moose Nostrils . . ."

"Thank you very much."

"Moose Nostrils . . ."

"Thank you very much."

Jesse Highboy was as excited out in the lobby as he'd been when the final buzzer sounded and they'd pounced on poor Jeremy to congratulate him.

He came straight over to Travis. "My dad says we can go out to the goose camp and stay overnight. He'll let us take the Ski-Doos."

Travis was taken aback. Ever since he'd arrived in Waskaganish he'd been hoping for a ride on one of the snow machines. But only a ride – he'd never considered driving. But then, he was from down South.

"All by ourselves?" Travis asked, a bit uneasily.

"My grandparents have been there for two weeks already. They'll be starting to hunt today. You gotta see it, Travis. It's a fantastic experience."

"It's all right with your grandparents?"

"My dad talked to them this morning. They saw the geese too."

"They have a telephone out there?"

Jesse laughed. "No way. A radio. We radioed them."

"I don't know," Travis said. He was suddenly unsure.

"My dad already asked your dad. There's no problem. I know the way. And my cousin Rachel's coming too. You know Rachel."

She was coming too?

"She's bringing Liz from your team. Liz is

staying with Rachel, and they've become good friends."

"How long does it take to get there?"

"Two hours. C'mon, let's clear it with Muck."

Muck listened carefully and then excused himself to go off and talk to Jesse's father. The two of them then spoke to Travis's and Liz's parents. The boys could see them talking, and were happy that heads were nodding in agreement. It seemed, however, to be taking an awfully long time.

Muck came back and said they could all go – on two conditions.

"What are they?" Travis asked.

"One, you get back here first thing in the morning. We play tomorrow at five p.m. I don't need tired players."

"We'll be back," Jesse promised.

"And two," Muck said, "you take Nishikawa with you."

Travis didn't understand. Or maybe he did. He looked at Muck, and Muck looked at both boys.

"He needs to open his eyes up here," Muck said. "And if he won't do it, we'll just have to do it for him."

7

TRAVIS HAD NEVER FELT ANYTHING LIKE IT! IT WAS as if he were surging right through his skin and leaving his body behind.

G-force. He only knew what it was because Data, the *Star Trek* freak, always talked about things like G-force and warp factor. You felt G-force in jet fighters and helicopters, and, Travis now knew, on very fast Ski-Doos.

Jesse's older brother, Isaac, had brought them out to show how to operate the machines they'd be taking to the goose camp. There were three: two larger machines pulling toboggans, and one smaller but quicker one.

Nish had reacted with what seemed like shock at the news that he was going. He obviously didn't want to seem *afraid* to go, but he didn't mind letting Travis know he was *reluctant*. He'd said he couldn't possibly go without his parents' permission, and when Muck had countered that by saying he had already called them from the band office and they thought it was a wonderful opportunity, he gave in and said he *guessed* he'd go. He was treating it like an extra practice Muck had scheduled.

Travis, on the other hand, could hardly wait. He was most excited by the chance to drive one of the Ski-Doos, and had eagerly taken up Isaac's offer to show him how. They had gone down on the bay to practice. It was flat and safe from trees and banks, and Isaac, sitting directly behind him, had called out, "*Open her up!*" and Travis had squeezed the accelerator.

The machine leapt from the ground. Travis felt airborne, his neck snapping back into the massive snowmobile helmet. The machine screamed down the shoreline, on a well-worn racing course that turned into a long, gentle curve. Travis tried to take the turn, but the machine skipped over the slight bank and began heading straight out into the bay, the pitch-black terror of open water far out in front. He let go of the accelerator, the machine slowed, and he could hear Isaac laughing.

"You have to *lean* into your turns!" Isaac told him. Then, with Travis now hanging on behind, Isaac drove the Ski-Doo back into the same curve, only this time leaning into the turn, with the machine following his coaxing. Travis took it for the run back, leaning just as Isaac had shown him, and the heavy slapping on his back from his passenger told him he'd done well. Travis felt great.

Jesse's father had spent the morning getting them ready to go. Five kids, three snow machines, two toboggans. The covered toboggans were filled with things like sleeping bags for the kids and extra supplies for the camp. As soon as the hockey tournament was over, the Highboys would be heading out for a two-week stay at the camp.

"Bring your stick and skates!" Jesse called to Travis and Nish as they went to pack. "There's sometimes good ice out by the goose blinds. If it's clear, we'll play some shinny."

"Sounds good!" Travis called back.

"Sounds stupid," Nish said as they continued toward the Highboy home to get their stuff.

"What do you mean, 'Sounds stupid'?" asked Travis.

"Where'll we dress? What'll we use for boards? Nets? Who's going to play? Us against the *girl*?"

What *was* it with Nish? From the moment they'd left Val d'Or, he had been in a sour mood. He hadn't said anything about Liz coming, and *she* was a girl. It was hardly like Nish to dump on someone just because they happened to be female. He wouldn't even use Rachel's name.

Nish didn't seem to like it that Travis and Rachel were getting along so well. The other night when they'd been lying in bed and Travis had been asking Jesse some perfectly reasonable questions — like how old she was, and in what grade, and what kind of music she liked — Nish had given a huge sigh and then made a big thing out of turning his back on them.

"Why don't you guys shut up so I can get some sleep?" he'd said angrily.

They got away by noon. Plenty of time, Mr. Highboy told them, to get there in good light and get settled in. Travis's and Liz's parents came down and took photographs of the expedition setting out. Travis's mother seemed worried, and he suddenly felt a little uneasy. But it was silly to fret, he told himself. They had three machines, so it would hardly matter if one broke down. They were dressed warmly and had big mittens and padded helmets. Jesse's father was a fanatic about taking all the right precautions, and there was going to be no fooling around.

Muck was there, too, and he took the three of them aside for a moment. "You stick together," he said to Nish and Travis and Liz. "And you do what Jesse and Rachel tell you, understand?" Nish clearly did not. He was, after all, an assistant captain, and Jesse was a third-liner. But having already fallen out once with Muck, he wasn't about to make a second mistake. Nish nodded.

Travis got to drive right away, with Nish as his passenger. They followed Jesse and Liz, who took the lead, and Rachel brought up the rear with the single snow machine.

They left the shoreline and headed into the

woods, where the trail began to bounce and roll with a rhythm that reminded Travis of riding a horse. It was never like this in a car. He could feel everything, and he loved it. A light squeeze of the accelerator and the big machine responded instantly.

They rolled over the countryside for the better part of an hour. They passed over frozen lakes and swamps and through short, dark stands of black spruce – and every once in a while they would catch a glimpse of the bay itself, the dark, menacing water far out from the shoreline.

They stopped to share a couple of oranges, and Nish complained to Jesse that he wasn't getting a chance to drive. Jesse immediately offered him the single machine, moving Rachel up to ride with Travis.

"Do you want to drive?" Travis asked when she moved over.

"You drive," Rachel said. "I can do it any time. You're only here until Sunday."

She smiled at him so nicely that, when she sat down behind him, Travis had trouble catching his breath. And when they moved on again and she placed her mittened hands on his hips to steady herself, he wondered if his heart would stop.

There was no use talking. With the helmets and the roar of the engine, they wouldn't hear each other. And anyway, that was just as well; Travis didn't have a clue what to talk about. Much-Music? Whether Rachel owned a compact-disc player? What did they talk about in the North?

They moved down a gentle slope and back to the shoreline of the big bay, the ice thick and covered with hard-packed snow, the trail perfect. In front, Jesse opened his machine up a bit and pulled ahead. Travis squeezed the accelerator and felt Rachel grip a little tighter. He felt wonderful. He had never in his entire life enjoyed anything as much as this.

Travis saw Nish before he heard him. His helmet blocked the sound and the engines of the three machines were all screaming together as Nish left the trail and flew past them with a wave of his hand.

Travis couldn't believe how fast Nish was going. Nish turned the machine so it jumped across the trail in front of Jesse and then continued on the other side, leaving them far behind.

"HE DOESN'T EVEN KNOW WHERE HE'S GOING!" Travis shouted. It was useless.

Nish let up on his accelerator until he had fallen back with them. Maybe he scared himself, thought Travis. But a moment later he was off the trail and flying away again, far out onto the frozen surface of the bay, the black, open water in the distance beyond him.

Travis couldn't help himself. "DON'T GO OUT THERE!"

He felt Rachel's grip tighten. Perhaps she was yelling too. But they couldn't even hear each other, so how would Nish ever hear them?

Jesse turned his machine off the trail and started out onto the bay, where Nish was in the middle of a long loop. Then Jesse came to a stop, jumped off, and began waving frantically to Nish. Travis stopped his machine.

The four of them – Jesse, Liz, Travis, and Rachel – all began waving at Nish. Travis thought that Nish must have been trying to turn back, but he wasn't leaning out the way Isaac had taught them, and the machine wasn't responding. Nish smashed into a drift and for a moment was airborne, the snowmobile almost turning sideways before he righted it and bounced into a landing that almost threw him off. Travis didn't need to be there to know that Nish had just scared himself half to death.

And then Nish vanished!

8

"NOOOOOO!!"

Travis was aware of the scream before he realized that it was him doing the screaming. He instinctively yanked his helmet free and started running, only to find he was going nowhere; someone had hold of him.

"YOU'LL GO THROUGH, TOO!" Rachel was shouting at him.

It was all too much for Travis. The screaming. The cold wind whipping in off the bay into his face. And a great dark hole where a moment before had been his best friend.

Travis panicked. He started to cry. He could feel tears burning. He looked at Liz. She was screaming.

Something bobbed in the water! Something surfacing. A head. An arm, flailing!

It was Nish!

Travis tried to move forward again, but Rachel was still holding him tight. He tried to shake her off, but Jesse grabbed him too.

"Cool it, okay?" Jesse shouted. "We panic, we're all going down with him. We do this right, okay? We do it right!"

Travis had never heard Jesse like this. He was so sure of himself. He stopped struggling.

Nish's helmet must have come off when the machine broke through the ice, because his head was bare – and he was *swimming*. Or at least trying to swim. With his heavy jacket and mitts, he could hardly move. But he managed to reach the unbroken ice and clung on.

"HELLLLLP MEEEE!!" he screamed.

Travis could feel his tears hardening on his cheek. They were freezing! It was that cold – and the wind was stronger now.

"Spread out!" Jesse ordered. "Spread out and walk slowly toward him! If we go in a single line we'll break through!"

Jesse got them into position, and they began walking in a wedge, Jesse in the lead, toward Nish, who was desperately hanging on.

"PULL ME OUT! PULLL MEEE OUTTT!!"

Rachel broke away and ran back. Travis couldn't look at her. She must have been afraid. He couldn't blame her – so was he. But before they were halfway to where Nish was still scrambling, she was back. She was carrying hockey sticks and skates. *What the heck's with her?* Travis wondered. *Nish is drowning and she wants to play hockey?*

"Good idea, Rach," Jesse said.

Travis couldn't believe the calm in Jesse's voice. What "good idea"?

"HELLLLLP MEEEE!!" Nish called again.

They were close enough to see his face when Jesse held up his hand for them all to stop. Travis could see the terror in Nish's eyes. He knew just from looking that Nish believed he was going to die, drown before their eyes while they stood there, watching helplessly.

There was desperation and anger in Nish's voice. "HELLLLLP MEEEE!!"

Nish tried to scramble onto the ice, but it shattered in front of him, plunging him down in a splash of ice-water. He bobbed back up, his hair plastered to his head. "PLEASE, HELP ME, TRAVIS!!"

"Hang on, Nish!" Jesse called. "We're gonna get you outta there! Just hold on and don't try to pull yourself up! You're breaking the ice!"

"HELLLLLP MEEEE!! I'M GONNA DIE!"

Signalling them to stay back, Jesse tested the ice by stepping ahead gently, then pressing down, waiting, and bringing the other foot forward and setting it down in the same careful way far to one side. He was slowly working his way as close to the hole as he dared get.

Travis looked around, desperate for something to do to help. Rachel was sitting on the ice with the hockey sticks placed together. She was unlacing one of the skates as quickly as possible.

She looked up, her face calm but determined. "Do the other ones," she commanded.

"Huh?"

"The other skates. We need the laces."

Travis and Liz began furiously unlacing the other skates. By the time they handed the laces to Rachel, she had already tied two hockey sticks together. She took Travis's lace and began tying another knot higher up for added support. Liz jumped over and began doing the same thing with her lace. Liz knew what to do. Travis could only stare uselessly.

Nish screamed the most terrible, pitiful scream. It was bloodcurdling. Travis shivered. He was still crying. He could feel his cheeks burning. He couldn't even see straight. His best friend was drowning and he couldn't do anything about it.

"Hold onto my legs!" Jesse shouted at Travis.

"What?"

"Hold onto my legs!" He repeated. He sounded angry.

Jesse lay down on his stomach and wiggled forward toward Nish. He looked back impatiently. Travis grabbed Jesse's legs, and when Jesse wiggled ahead again Travis moved with him.

Nish was still trying to pull himself up. He was breaking through and falling back.

"Stay still!" Jesse ordered Nish. "You might break right through to us!"

There was so much command in his voice that, finally, Nish stopped struggling.

Jesse looked back at Rachel, who was ready. She handed the sticks forward to him. Jesse swung them carefully out in front. He was at least one hockey stick short of Nish.

"We're gonna have to get closer!"

Travis didn't know if they could. He was afraid of breaking through. His heart was pounding so hard it seemed to be shaking his whole body. He could imagine his parents finding out that they'd all vanished on the bay, with nothing remaining but two snowmobiles and a big black hole. They wouldn't even know how it had happened, that Nish had been such a dummy.

He felt someone grab his own legs. He looked back. It was Rachel, and behind her Liz was down with her arms around Rachel's legs.

"Go on!" Rachel shouted ahead to Jesse. "We can hold you!"

Jesse wiggled forward. Travis wriggled. The girls wriggled. They moved ahead like a slow snake, the blade of the farthest stick coming ever closer to Nish.

"Grab it and hold!" Jesse shouted to Nish. "Don't pull! We'll do all the pulling! You just hold on and try to slide out, okay?"

Nish was no longer screaming. He was scared. He was placing all his hope in Jesse.

"O-k-kay!" Nish said. He was crying openly. Travis couldn't blame him. He was crying too.

Jesse wiggled ahead one more time. Nish reached out with one mitt and took hold of the blade. He had a good grip.

"Let go of the ice!" Jesse called.

"I CAN'T!" Nish shouted. There was pure terror in his voice.

"You have to!"

"I'M AFRAID TO LET GO!"

Suddenly, from behind Travis, Rachel shouted, "LET GO, NISH! YOU'LL BE ALL RIGHT!"

There was a brief pause, and then Nish let go of the ice and took the blade with both hands.

"Hang on!" Jesse shouted. Then, to Travis and the others, "Slowly, now. Pull back slowly!"

They began to inch backwards.

Nish pushed at the ice. It cracked loudly and gave under him, sending him back down.

"JUST RIDE RIGHT OVER THE ICE!" Jesse yelled. "DON'T DO A THING BUT HANG ON AND SLIDE!"

They pulled again, and Nish came out part way. The ice gave a mighty crack and Travis closed his eyes – but nothing happened. It was holding.

They pulled again. Nish came up a bit more. His upper body was out and resting on the ice. His face was twisted into a scream, but no sound was coming out.

"ONE MORE!" Jesse called. "ONE MORE AND HE'S OUT!"

Travis felt a tremendous yank on his legs. He couldn't believe the strength of the two girls behind him. He pulled as hard as he could. He could feel Jesse pulling.

"HE'S OUT!"

Jesse turned over on his back, gasping for air. Nish was fully out of the water and on the ice. He was wiggling toward them, still holding the stick.

They worked Nish back. As soon as he was able, Jesse reached out, grabbed Nish's hands, and pulled him quickly to them.

"Spread out again!" Jesse ordered. "We don't want to break through!"

Travis moved away quickly. Nish tried to get to his feet. He was gasping, choking, and shaking violently. Jesse stayed with him, got him standing, and slowly they all began retreating from the hole.

Nish was bawling. He couldn't stop. He was sobbing and blubbering and couldn't seem to get his breath. But he was alive!

Though how long could he last before he froze to death? Travis wondered.

9

TRAVIS HAD NEVER FELT SO HELPLESS. IF HE HAD been in charge, Nish and he would have turned to ice on the banks of James Bay, their frozen tears proof that they had been bawling like newborn babies right to the bitter end.

Fortunately, Travis wasn't in charge – Jesse and Rachel Highboy were. Jesse opened up the lead toboggan and removed one of the sleeping bags, which he quickly unrolled and wrapped around the shaking, whimpering Nish.

"We've got to get out of the wind," Jesse said. There was no panic in his voice, just grim determination.

Jesse wasted no time. He got Nish onto the lead Ski-Doo with him, Rachel and Liz took the other one, and Travis straddled the toboggan. Jesse quickly found a trail up from the shore, and as Rachel followed, Travis took one last look behind him. The bay was quickly vanishing from view, but above it he could see a huge, threatening cloud the colour of a bad bruise. He hoped it was going away from them.

The two machines entered a thick stand of

spruce, and Travis could see Jesse standing up as he drove, his helmeted head turning this way and that, until finally he came to a clearing surrounded by trees. He stopped his machine, and Rachel pulled hers up directly behind.

"Keep Nish warm!" Jesse shouted to Travis as he began opening up the two toboggans.

Travis could see his friend was shaking right through the sleeping bag. What was he supposed to do? Turn up the thermostat?

"*Rub him!*" Jesse shouted. He already had an axe out, and was throwing other things onto the ground. Out came a big orange plastic sheet, another axe, a shovel. Rachel took the shovel and began to make a bank of snow around a small area within the clearing.

Travis and Liz felt stupid and useless. Travis shrugged at Liz, wrapped his arms around Nish, and began rubbing him through the covers. He could feel his best friend shaking – no, *rattling* – like a machine that was about to burst apart. Travis was scared. Liz moved in to wrap her arms around Nish, too.

"LEMME BREATHE!" Nish shouted. It was like music to Travis's ears. At least Nish was still Nish. Frozen, maybe, but still Nish.

While Liz and Travis rubbed the freezing Nish, Rachel continued banking up the snow. Then she snapped off dead branches from the spruce trees and set about making a fire. She carefully laid down the dry wood, crisscrossing the branches, then returned to the spruce for some live boughs with needles still on them.

With what seemed like a dozen quick chops with the axe, Jesse had felled one of the spruce trees. He lopped off some of the branches, then pulled a small Swedesaw from the toboggan and quickly set to work cutting up the trunk. Travis could see the sweat pouring off Jesse's forehead.

When he had cut three good-sized pieces, Jesse knelt down in the snow and chopped at each one until he had dozens of long, curling chips that were only half cut away from the logs. Travis had no idea what he was doing.

Rachel started the fire. The dry branches caught easily, and then the needles ignited, the fire roaring and snapping almost as if she had poured gasoline on it. As soon as it was really going, Jesse piled on his three logs, and Travis saw now why he had cut them the way he had. The long, curling chips sticking out from the logs caught fire easily, and not only did they help the fire grow stronger, they kept the logs apart so the flames could lick up in between. Jesse had no time to admire his work: he was right back sawing more logs from the downed spruce.

Rachel had the other axe and was cutting down smaller trees. The axe was so sharp, some fell with one or two blows, until Rachel had nearly a dozen down and was busy hacking off the branches. It looked to Travis as if she was making fishing poles.

"I-I-I th-th-th-ink I-I'm dyyy-inggg!" Nish suddenly howled. He sounded like a sick dog.

"Don't be ridiculous!" Liz snapped at him.

She, too, seemed suddenly in control. In fact, everyone appeared to know what to do but Nish, who thought he was dying, and Travis, who thought he was useless.

Rachel was working the poles into the snow to one side of the fire. "Travis!" she called. "Can you help me for a minute?"

Travis had hold of Nish and was afraid to let go. But Liz pushed him off and hugged Nish closer. Travis hurried over.

"Help me get these up!" Rachel told him. "They'll have to hold against the wind."

Travis followed Rachel's instructions exactly. They pounded the poles down like fenceposts in a semi-circle, and then built up more snow around them. Rachel had planned her structure so it included three live spruce, their roots holding them far more solid than anything Travis and Rachel could manage by pounding. She cleared off their branches with the axe so that the standing spruce fit perfectly in line, one on each end and one in the middle.

Travis still had no idea what she was doing.

"Help us with the tarp!" she called. She and

Jesse were already unrolling the big orange plastic sheet. The three of them hoisted the tarp up and, using bungee cords, carefully attached it flat against the spruce posts. Rachel and Jesse took special care to secure it to the three spruce trees that still had their roots. When they were done, they had built a wall that curved in a semi-circle, which not only cut off the wind but also caught the heat of the fire. Travis could feel the heat blasting at him. It felt wonderful.

Neither Rachel nor Jesse had spoken a word to each other during the whole procedure. They had called out instructions to Travis and Liz, but nothing whatsoever to each other. Had they practised this in case some idiot fell through the ice? Travis wondered.

But there was no time for foolish questions.

Jesse remained in control, though he still looked concerned. "Get that sleeping bag off Nish!" he commanded, coming over to help. Nish whimpered and held tight to his covers.

Jesse was almost angry. "You *will* die if we don't get you dried out!" he said in a very firm voice. "Now let go!"

Once Nish was out of the sleeping bags, Travis could see how much his friend was shaking – and it scared him. His jacket, his pants, everything was absolutely soaking.

"Off with the clothes!" Jesse commanded.

"I-I-I'll freeeeze!"

"You'll freeze if you don't. C'mon. This is no time for modesty. Get 'em off."

With Jesse's help, Nish began taking off his stuff. As each item was removed, Rachel gathered the wet clothing up and carefully hung it to dry on spruce branches she had arranged around the fire.

Travis was shocked at the sight of his friend. They were in the middle of nowhere, in freezing cold, with an Arctic wind, and Nish stood there naked like a beached whale, almost a blur he shook so badly. Jesse got a dry sleeping bag from the toboggan and gave it to Nish to wrap around himself.

"Travis," Jesse called, "break into his pack. Get us some dry clothes."

Travis was thankful he finally had something to do. He hurried to the second toboggan and pulled out Nish's pack. He quickly undid the straps and untied the cord. Then he stopped, blinking in astonishment.

The pack was filled with candy! Mars bars and Caramilk and Snickers and licorice and bubble gum and Gummi bears and Reeses and Smarties and a six-pack of Coke. All Travis could find for Nish to wear was a fresh pair of boxer shorts and a sweatshirt.

Travis took the clothes back, holding them out as if he had failed. "This is all he brought."

"I–I thought w–we were st–staying only th–the one night!" said Nish.

Then why bring enough candy for a month? Travis wanted to say, but bit his tongue.

Jesse shook his head in disgust. "Okay, put 'em on!"

"P–put what on?"

"Put 'em on!" Jesse ordered again. There was no mistaking what he meant; he was holding out the boxer shorts. He wasn't taking no for an answer.

Whimpering, Nish started to change. He pulled the dry sleeping bag tight and stepped out of his wet shorts, kicking them aside with an alarmingly white foot. *Was it frozen?*

"Travis 'n' me are too small," Jesse said. "Have you got anything he can wear, Liz?"

"I'll check," Liz said, and hurried to her own pack.

Nish howled like a dog who'd just had his tail run over. He was halfway up with his dry underwear and the sleeping bag slipped off.

"*I can't wear girls' clothes!*"

"Right," Jesse said. "Then they can all say, 'Good ol' Nish – he froze to death like a *real* man.'"

"How's this?" Liz said. She was holding a thick pink sweater, a pair of black tights, some thick socks, and a pair of blue jeans with some bead-work on the back pockets.

"*T–t–tights!*" Nish wailed.

"Put them on," Rachel said. Even she was losing her patience. "Put them on or freeze your buns off."

Nish accepted the bundle. He began to dress, whimpering still; but whether it was because he thought he was going to die from freezing or from embarrassment, Travis could not say.

Jesse returned to the job of cutting up wood, and Travis went to help him. They cut more logs and stacked them, and Travis gathered more dry branches. The fire was going well.

"You look lovely!" Rachel said as Nish emerged from his sleeping bag.

Liz's clothes didn't fit quite perfectly, but at least Nish could wear them. The pink sweater was okay, but the pants he couldn't quite do up, and they could see the tights through the zipper. The beads sparkled in the firelight as Nish warmed his behind.

Jesse and Rachel still weren't finished. They pulled another plastic tarp out of the toboggan and used it to make a partial roof over the shelter. On the enclosed side it was now so warm Travis could hardly believe it. Rachel cut down some soft spruce boughs and spread them around so they could sit and not get wet or cold from the snow.

Nish was no longer shaking. His clothes were steaming beside the fire. The wind was higher now, and rippling loudly along the outside of the plastic tarp.

"We're in for a storm," said Jesse, very quietly.

"I think so," answered Rachel.

Travis didn't like their near-whispers. It was almost as if they were warning each other, but didn't want the rest to know. He stared toward the bay. He could see nothing but a blur. It was snowing, hard – and coming their way.

Jesse shook his head, seemingly angry with himself. "If only I'd packed some food."

"There's nothing?" Rachel asked.

Jesse shook his head. "I figured we'd get there easily before dark. They'd already have geese."

"We've got something," Travis said.

All heads turned toward him, including Nish, who couldn't contain a look of alarm.

"Nish brought his candy," Travis said.

Nish stared at him with a look that said: *How could you betray your best friend?*

"Let's have a look," said Liz.

Travis hauled out the bag and opened it. Rachel giggled when she saw the enormous cache of sweets. Jesse just shook his head.

"Stuff like that attracts bears, you know, Nish," he said.

"There's no bears around here, are there?"

"You better hope not."

10

THEY HAD A THREE–COURSE SUPPER. LICORICE AS AN appetizer, Mars bars and Snickers for the main course, bubble gum for dessert. And all washed down with Coke.

"We'll open two cans and share," said Jesse.

"I'm not touching it after someone else," protested Nish.

"Suit yourself," said Jesse. "But we have no idea how long we'll be here."

"We can eat snow," Nish suggested.

"People die eating snow. You have to melt it first – so save the cans."

Travis had never seen this side of Jesse. Usually Jesse hardly said a word; he always let others take the lead and simply followed along. But now he was in charge. Captain, sort of, of the lost team.

They kept the fire going and talked. Travis asked about Jesse kneeling when he chopped with the axe, and Jesse explained to him that all the Cree did this. "You live in the bush, you can't take a chance on cutting your foot," he said. "You'd never get to help in time."

Nish was warm finally, and most of his clothes were dry. He wrapped himself up again in the sleeping bag, changed back into his own clothes, and sheepishly handed Liz hers back with an awkward "Thanks."

"Any time, cross-dresser," said Liz.

Nish squinted and frowned at the same time. "Not one word of this to the others, okay?"

"Of course not."

"Good."

"How could *one* word describe you?"

They all laughed, until a great burst of wind suddenly hit the shelter and snapped the plastic, bending the poles.

"It's really gonna blow," said Jesse.

"They'll be wondering where we are," said Liz.

"They'll know where we are," said Jesse. He seemed certain.

Later, Jesse and Rachel got up to arrange the snowmobiles and toboggans so that they gave more shelter as the kids huddled into the best corner of the wall they had built. They were fairly comfortable – out of the wind and snow, each one wrapped in an Arctic sleeping bag, lying on soft boughs over the snow – but they were also miserable, and badly frightened.

Travis had never seen such a storm. It seemed to howl and pounce like an animal, the air growing eerily quiet and then suddenly rising and punching the tarp so they felt it would rip off and come down on them. But Rachel had done a good job; the tarp held. And Jesse had cut and stacked enough wood for the fire to burn forever.

But they were still cold. Cold and hungry, despite the chocolate bars and licorice. Travis felt ill from all the sugar. Nish was making funny gurgling noises. Travis realized he was crying, very softly, to himself.

"What's wrong?" he asked.

"I lost the Ski-Doo," Nish said.

"It's not important," Jesse said.

"It's my fault," Nish said.

"That's right," Jesse said. Travis had the sense that this wasn't what Nish was hoping to hear. "But it would have been my fault if we'd lost you."

"And mine," Rachel added.

"How?" Nish moaned.

"We're responsible for you," said Jesse.

"Our grandparents would say you are guests in their home," said Rachel. "So if something does go wrong, it's up to us to fix it."

"But we're not in their home, we're in the middle of the bush," corrected Travis.

"*This*," she said, "is our grandparents' home."

11

MUCK AND MR. LINDSAY WERE IN THE BAND OFFICE
with Mr. Highboy and Chief Ottereyes. The
storm had come up very suddenly – "It happens
sometimes," said the Chief. They had radioed the
Highboy goose camp, but the grandparents had
seen no sign of the five youngsters yet.

Both the Chief and Mr. Highboy said not to
worry, and didn't seem particularly worried
themselves, but Muck and Mr. Lindsay were
definitely worried.

"Jesse knows what to do," Mr. Highboy kept
saying. "Jesse and Rachel know the bush."

Abraham and Hilda Highboy had known the
storm was on its way since shortly after noon.
Abraham had heard the wind in the high trees
and knew. They considered radioing the village
to let them know, but it was Rachel and Jesse
coming out. They'd be okay.

Hilda had been in the cooking tent since
morning. She had a huge fire going and she had
four geese trussed and hanging from the main

poles out over the centre, where they were spinning on their tie lines and sizzling in the waves of rising heat. Every once in a while she would take a bowl and catch the grease drippings. Perfect for bannock, she said to herself. The kids would be hungry when they arrived.

Abraham had skinned a beaver he had trapped the day before and had stretched the pelt for curing outside. The beaver meat was cooking in a slow pot held high over the main campfire. The entire camp smelled of food. But it was not the cooking smells that were making Abraham's nose twitch. He did not like the smell of the wind bearing down on them, gusting direct from the north, the temperature dropping.

Even the dogs were uneasy. Abraham was one of the last Waskaganish trappers still working with sled dogs. He could have bought a Ski-Doo, but he stuck with the dogs because he had always loved working with them, and, besides, what could a snow machine ever tell you? The dogs were letting him know the storm was a bad one. They were nervous, and selfish. He had noticed them fighting over the meat; a storm like this made everyone, man or dog, think survival. The only thing good about the temperature going down further was that soon it would be too cold to snow. Soon, he figured, he would be able to see enough to travel in the dark. If he had to.

12

NISH WAS SURE HE'D HEARD SOMETHING. AND IT wasn't just Jesse up again to stoke the fire: this sound had come from outside the shelter.

He hadn't been able to sleep. He could hear Travis snoring. He could make out the girls huddled against each other. He could see Jesse closer to the fire, his face turned toward it.

The fire was crackling. Rachel had explained that it was caused by the resin in the spruce. It was spitting and sizzling and snapping . . . *snapping?*

No, the snapping was coming from outside! Nish held his breath.

Snap!

Something was moving through the trees!

Nish could feel his heart pounding. The wind kicked the sides of the plastic tarp and it rattled and rippled the entire length.

Snap!

"*Trav!*" Nish hissed.

No answer.

"*Jesse!*"

No answer.

"*Rachel! . . . Liz!*"

Nothing.

Nish didn't know what to do. He didn't want to shout for fear of alerting whatever it was on the other side of the tarp. He also had to go to the bathroom – *bad*. Too much Coke.

Quietly, barely daring to breathe, Nish waited. He counted to a hundred, then to two hundred. He was desperate, now, to go to the bathroom. Three hundred. Four hundred. *He had to go!*

Satisfied that whatever it was had moved along, he quickly pulled himself out of the sleeping bag. It was freezing cold – particularly for a twelve-year-old about to unbuckle his pants!

Nish stepped around the edge of the shelter. He'd go so quick, he figured, the hole in the snow would be like a bullet had passed through. But he never even got to try.

Something was breathing nearby . . . something big!

Nish was shaking. He could see nothing but pitch black around him. The trees were like huge shadows, with darker shadows below them. *And one of the shadows was moving!* He could hear growling, and snarling!

"*Uhhhhhh!*" Nish started. He didn't dare move.

He could see eyes! At first he wasn't sure, then he saw them again, yellow, *shining*.

The thing lunged. He could hear the intake of breath, the growl. It hit him dead centre in the chest. Nish went down, gasping. He could smell the animal. Sharp, rancid, disgusting. He could smell its panting breath – hot, and fouler than anything he had ever smelled. Nish thought he was going to throw up.

He still couldn't see. He was down and the beast was striking him with its paws, the claws ripping into his arms and sides and tearing out his insides. He began to scream.

He screamed and gurgled, sure that it was blood rising in his throat. There was no pain . . . *yet*. But he knew he was badly injured, probably dying. All he could see was the burning eyes, all he could feel was harsh, thick fur, all he could smell was the foul, dead, disgusting smell.

Nish tried to move and could not. If his legs and arms were broken, he couldn't feel them. He could feel a terrible warmth on his stomach, a sickening warm sensation that could only be his own blood pouring out.

"I'm dying!"

He tried to warn the others, but they wouldn't wake. He could hear the tarp tearing as the beast ripped through it. He could hear snorting and ripping. He turned, barely, the warm liquid of his own insides cooling now. *So this*, he decided, *is what it feels like to die.*

He could see the beast dragging something. *It was Travis!* It had torn Travis out of his sleeping bag and was dragging him off.

"TRAAAAVIS!!!"

13

"*Nish! . . . Nish!*"

"*C'mon, Nish. Wake up!*"

Nish twisted, tried to open his eyes. He thought he must be in heaven, but it didn't make sense; God wouldn't call him by his nickname. He must be in a hospital. Somehow he must have been saved.

"*Nish, wake up!*"

That was . . . Travis's voice. Nish shook his head violently. A good sign: it didn't fall off. At least the beast hadn't ripped out his throat. But he couldn't tell if he could feel his legs, and the pool of blood on his stomach was freezing cold now.

"WAKE UP!"

Nish opened his eyes. Travis was leaning over him, shaking his shoulders. So Travis hadn't been eaten! Behind Travis, Nish could make out the others, all looking at him, concerned. And behind them – what *was* that? The *beast*? He could see something big, and dark, and covered with fur.

"Travis," Nish said, "you're okay?"

Travis laughed. "Of course I'm okay. It's you

we're worried about. Jesse's grandfather is here! We're saved, Nish!"

Saved? How could they be saved when a minute ago they were being eaten by a wild animal? He shifted so he could see creature. *It was an old man!* An old man with thick eyebrows and long greying hair, wearing a big fur coat. The old man looked more like a bear than . . . Jesse's grandfather. But that's who it was.

Nish could feel his legs now. And his arms. But he could still feel the wet where the beast had ripped out his guts.

Oh oh!

Nish closed his eyes. He knew.

He had gone to the bathroom last night all right. But he had never left his sleeping bag.

When the old trapper found them, the fire had gone down to nothing. Cree hunters had frozen to death in the past in a good shelter with a fire going: sleep had tricked them. When he first got there, with his dogs barking and nobody waking up, he had become quite worried.

As he told them later, with Jesse translating, he had tried to shake one kid awake. He pointed to Nish, laughing. Nish, he said, had started screaming at him. And then he had fainted. The old trapper said something and laughed to himself, shaking his head.

"My grandfather says you saw the Trickster," said Jesse.

"I saw an animal," Nish protested. "I think it was a wolverine."

"You wouldn't know a wolverine from a skunk," said Rachel, laughing.

"Get a life," Nish snapped.

"Get a diaper," said Rachel.

Nish shut up. What could he say? He'd made a complete ass of himself. They thought he was a scaredy-cat, a baby. And he'd done nothing to make them think otherwise. He'd lost the Ski-Doo through the ice; he'd almost drowned; he couldn't do a thing to help when they built the camp; and he'd peed his bed.

They all helped themselves to the meat that Jesse and Rachel's grandfather had brought. It was black and greasy – "Mostly goose, some beaver," Jesse had said – and it smelled . . . well, delicious, Nish thought. He took a nibble of what Jesse swore was goose, and it tasted wonderful. He took a second piece. It tasted even better.

They rode quickly to the goose camp. The wind was down, and the morning was, unbelievably, as beautiful as the day before when they had started out from the village. They looked like a gang out for a casual ride in the forest: two snow machines and a dog sled, nothing to show that they had nearly drowned, or frozen to death, or, for that matter, been attacked by the dreaded Trickster.

Travis got to ride on the dog sled with the grandfather. It was wonderful, if a bit slower than the Ski-Doos. The dogs barked and pulled, more with a series of yanks than with the steady drive of the machines, but it felt better. He could sense them surging, he could feel their joy as they got onto an open stretch of the bay. The sun was fully out now, and glistening where the ice had been swept clear of snow by the winds. There was no open water around here.

Travis thought about what had happened to them and how incredibly lucky they were. Lucky that Jesse and Rachel knew how to get someone out of the water and build a fire and a shelter. Lucky that the old man had found them.

Nish was still acting as if the dream was real, not something he had dreamt at all. Travis couldn't believe that Nish could have gone to the bathroom in his sleeping bag; he must have been truly terrified. He wondered why he hadn't had a bad dream himself. And then he remembered. *The dream catcher.* Rachel's present was in his pack. It was working!

The dogs began yelping and howling as they came closer to the island where the camp was. The snow machines had already arrived, and Jesse,

Rachel, and Liz were hurrying about, checking out the camp.

Jesse and Rachel's grandmother had all sorts of food laid out for them: bannock, caribou, goose, and big fat oatmeal cookies baked with the goose drippings she'd been collecting.

"I'm *starving!*" shouted Nish, and he began digging in. He winked at Travis.

Jesse radioed back to the village, and Travis, standing beside him, was sure he could hear whoops coming from someone who sounded a lot like Muck. He had never heard Muck whoop before, but he was still pretty sure it was him.

"We've all missed games," Jesse said when he turned off the radio. "Rachel's team won this morning."

"*All right!*" shouted Rachel. "*Go Wolverines!*"

"We can't get back in time for our game against the Northern Lights," said Jesse. "My dad and some others are coming, but they can't be here until at least two o'clock."

"What'll we do?" asked Nish.

"Play hockey," Jesse said.

"Yeah!" agreed Rachel.

"Whadya mean?" Nish thought they were still making fun of him.

"Didn't you see the ice on the way out here?" Rachel asked. "It's better than Maple Leaf Gardens!"

"And a hundred times as big!" Jesse added.

14

TRAVIS LIKED TO THINK OF HIMSELF AS A BIT OF AN expert on ice conditions and hockey rinks, but he had never seen, or felt, anything quite like this.

Until now, he had always believed he liked the ice at the beginning of a game best, when it seemed a puck might slide forever. He liked the way he could kick his ankles out on a corner and shoot up a quick spray of ice with nothing more than a flick of his skate blade.

But now he liked new ice in an arena second best. *This*, he told himself, was special. The howling wind of the night before had cleared the narrows between the island and the shore. The surface was smooth as polished marble.

It was the hardness that delighted Travis the most. Once he put on his skates and set out, he found the noise of his blades astonishing. It was as if someone had turned up the volume.

There was a light wind and, when he went with it, it seemed he was flying even faster than Dmitri. With the skates making a sharp rasp on the ice, he could turn in an instant, the ice so hard and the skates so sharp that there was simply no play in the two at all. Instant response.

They were all out there now. All in their team jackets, different coloured toques, pants, gloves. They threw down a puck and began rapping it back and forth, the sound much louder than in an enclosed arena. It sounded like music to Travis.

"*Let's have a game!*" Jesse shouted.

"*Uneven numbers!*" Travis called back.

There were five of them out on the ice: Jesse, Travis, Liz, Rachel, Nish. They'd have to go three-on-two.

"Where'll we play?" Nish asked. The others all laughed, but he shook his head violently. "No, I'm serious – where?"

"*Wherever we want!*" Liz shouted.

"I'll get some posts," Rachel said.

Rachel skated back toward the camp. Travis could see the grandparents outside, down by the shoreline. They were piling a toboggan high with a variety of goose decoys, some of them the modern plastic kind from the South, most of them original Cree style, made from tamarack twigs tied together to fashion a head, long neck, and plump body.

Jesse and Rachel came back, each carrying two of the large plastic geese. Rachel dumped hers close to the other kids, while Jesse skated farther down the ice with his two.

"Goal posts," she announced as she began setting them upright.

"We've still got uneven numbers," said Travis.

"Grandpa's going to play. It's North against South."

Nish couldn't believe it. "Your *grandfather?*"

Rachel smiled. "It's *his* rink!"

Travis had never even imagined a game like this. No boards, the ice going on forever, goose decoys for goalposts, a switch at halftime because of the wind, *and a goaltender with a shovel!*

There was nothing else for the old man to play with. He didn't seem to mind. He dropped it off his shoulder and plonked it down onto the ice. Then he shoved it hard into Travis's stick and dislodged the puck. The old man laughed. "Hockey," he said.

"Hey!" Nish shouted to Jesse. "Your grandfather can speak English!"

"He can't," said Jesse, laughing. "There's just no Cree word for the game."

They split up into teams, and Travis, Liz, and Nish went down to their own goal, carrying the puck. They gathered for a moment.

"Go easy on them," Travis said. "We don't want the old man falling down or anything."

"Let's go!" shouted Nish.

Travis lugged the puck out a way, then dropped it back to Nish. Nish tried to hit Travis as he broke, but the puck was behind him and shot away, nearly all the way to the island.

"Go get it!" Rachel laughed. "You missed it."

"Now you're finding out why Crees always complete their passes," Jesse called after him.

Travis couldn't believe how far the puck had travelled. Maybe Jesse was right: play here every day and you'd never take a stupid chance. And come to think of it, Jesse's one great strength was the accuracy of his passing.

Travis brought the puck back and lobbed a long pass to Liz, who skated easily with it and then dropped it back to Nish. With Rachel chasing him, Nish dumped the puck out to the middle, where Travis picked it up in full flight. He took Jesse with him toward the island, then let a soft backhand go for Liz, who went in on the old man, *only to have him poke-check her perfectly with the shovel!*

"No fair!" Nish called from behind.

"Whadya mean, 'No fair'?" Jesse demanded.

"How are we supposed to get by a shovel?"

"Wait till you see him rush with the puck!" Rachel laughed.

"Huh?" Nish said, then realized she was kidding.

Jesse carried the puck up, skating easily by Liz. He then passed to Rachel, who was coming up Travis's side. This was the first Travis had seen her skate. She was fast, very fast.

He cut her off, and when she tried to tuck the puck in under his stick, he used his skate to catch it and move it up onto his own stick. He was clear. Nothing between him and the Stanley Cup but an old man with a shovel.

Travis came down on the goal not knowing what to do. He couldn't get too close or the shovel would come out. He couldn't hoist – that would hardly be fair. And he couldn't just shoot a quick one along the ice: the shovel pretty well covered the whole net.

Travis decided to try the amazing move he'd been working on in practice but never dared try in a game, the one Muck kept shaking his head over. He came in, and Jesse's grandfather, laughing, went to the poke check. But just as the shovel moved toward the puck, Travis dropped the puck back so it clicked off first his right blade and then his left, and then, on an unsuspected angle, past the shovel and out the other side. Travis jumped over the shovel, home free, and tapped the puck between the geese.

He turned back and dropped instantly to his knees, spinning as he glided down the ice. He flipped his stick over, pretended to clean the shaft like a sword, and then made a motion as if he were sheathing his trusty blade.

"*Hot dog!*" Jesse shouted, laughing.

"*Muck should be here!*" Liz called. "*The famous move finally worked!*"

"Yeah," Rachel added, "on an old man with a shovel and no skates!"

Travis couldn't tell whether she was kidding him or insulting him. He had to admit it was a bit much. He didn't really know why he'd done it – the big turn, the drop to the knees, the stupid sword thing – but he had. He wanted Rachel to appreciate his terrific move. He wanted her to know what a good hockey player he was. Maybe he didn't know much about the bush, but he sure knew the game of hockey.

They played with no sense of score or time. They raced from end to end, the sounds of their skates as loud as their shouting, the ice flying, the skate blades flashing in the sun, the old man laughing as he stood his ground at the Cree net with his shovel and big hunting boots.

They played until they dropped, and then they went back to the camp, where the grandmother had another meal laid out. Only this time it wasn't goose. It was moose.

"Sorry, Nish," said Rachel as they sat down. "No nostrils, I'm afraid."

Nish scowled and held his plate out. He was too hungry to waste his breath taking shots at anyone. He took extra bannock.

"You haven't got any of that candy left, have you, Nish?" Jesse asked after they had eaten their fill. "We could do with some dessert."

Nish shook his head. "You guys ate it all."

"Come on outside," Rachel said, holding up a clean spoon. They looked at her like she was crazy. "Come on," she repeated. "Everybody."

The sun was still high, and they came out blinking in the strong light. They could see and hear the rescue mission from the village as the snowmobiles appeared along the far shore. They would be here in a few minutes.

Rachel went over to the closest snowbank. It was perfectly white, perfectly clean. She reached out and took a spoonful, blowing some of the fine powder off before turning to Travis.

"You want to try first?" she asked.

Travis didn't know what to say. Rachel had obviously heard the story about Christmas in the bush, but Travis didn't know whether she was making a fool of him or whether he was being given a great honour. When he saw the way she was smiling, he could only nod his head.

"Close your eyes," she said.

Travis closed his eyes.

"Open your mouth."

He opened his mouth.

The spoon rattled on his lower teeth. He could feel the cold of the metal. He closed his mouth over the soft, frozen snow and took it off the spoon. It seemed to explode on his tongue, the cold so sharp, tickling the roof of his mouth, the instant ice and water so refreshing. And almost ... yes, he had to admit it, almost *sweet*. Just like Jimmy Whiskeyjack's grandmother had said.

"Well?" he heard Rachel ask.

Travis opened his eyes, blinking in the brightness, surprised by how close she was to him. He could smell her, and she, too, smelled bright and sweet as the open air.

"Good," he said.

"You want to try, Liz?"

"Sure."

The grandparents were out, watching and laughing as if they knew the story, perhaps had done it themselves for their own children. Clapping her hands as if she'd just remembered something, the grandmother turned and hurried back into the camp.

Liz smacked her lips.

"Can I have seconds?" she laughed.

Rachel shook her head. "It's a once-in-a-lifetime experience. Nish?"

Nish shook his head. "No way."

"C'mon, Nish!" they called out. The grandmother came back out, giggling to herself.

"C'mon! Give it a try," Liz said.

Rachel nudged him: "It's good – you'll like it."

Nish shook his head, his mouth tightly clenched.

The old woman laughed and took the spoon from Rachel. She grasped Nish by the hand and led him to another bank, where the angle of the sun was now turning the snow the colour of gold. She reached out and took an enormous spoonful. She held it up, smiling.

Nish didn't know what to do. He couldn't say no; she didn't even speak his language. He couldn't be rude.

The grandmother began speaking Cree, almost as if she was singing. She reached up with her other hand and placed it over his eyes, so he would shut them tight.

Nish closed his eyes. He made a quick face and then opened his mouth wide.

Travis barely saw it happen. At first he wasn't sure what she had done, but it seemed the spoon with the snow in it had disappeared into the old woman's pocket and another spoon was suddenly in her hand. Only this one had been dipped in water and then into a sugar jar. It was covered in sugar crystals. She quickly passed the spoon over the snowbank to cover the sugar with a layer of snow.

Then she placed the spoon in Nish's mouth. He bit down, sucked a moment, then opened his eyes wide. Nish looked in total shock.

"Well?" said Rachel.

"I can't believe it," Nish said, his eyes big and black as hockey pucks. "*I can-not be-lieve it.*"

15

ALL THE WAY BACK TO THE VILLAGE, AND EVEN after they'd arrived, Nish kept repeating, "I can't believe it. I can not believe it."

Travis was amazed at the reception when they got back, the way the entire village once again turned out to greet them, including, this time, the rest of the Screech Owls, their parents, and the coaches.

The first figure they saw when they came within sight of Waskaganish was Muck. Growing impatient, he had walked out to meet them. He hugged them all, even Nish, and Muck never hugged anyone. Not even when they won the championship at Lake Placid.

Data and Andy and Chantal and Derek and Dmitri and Cherry and Gordie and all the rest of the Owls had been standing high on the snowbanks so they would see the snowmobiles come into view, and most of them ran down and out over the frozen bay to meet the lost Screech Owls as soon as they appeared, jogging alongside and cheering their return.

Nish sat like Santa Claus on the last float of the

parade, waving to each side. Travis wondered if it had occurred to Nish that this whole thing was taking place because of him.

"*We're in the final!*" Derek called as Travis's ride passed by him.

The Screech Owls had won their game against the Northern Lights, even without their best defenceman, their captain, and Jesse Highboy. And after all the wins and losses had been added up, and all the goals for and against accounted for, it was announced that the First Nations Pee Wee Hockey Tournament final would be played that evening: Screech Owls versus the Waskaganish Wolverines.

"*We made the final!*" Rachel shouted when she got the news. She pointed at Travis and Nish. "*We're* going to play *you* for the championship!"

"You won't have a prayer," Nish said.

"Why not?"

"Shovels are illegal."

●

Travis was out of sorts. He had dressed carefully for the final game, but he still didn't feel right. Mr. Dillinger had sharpened his skates perfectly. "Good gosh," he'd said when he looked along one of the blades, "what on earth were you doing with these, whittling wood?" Travis told Mr. Dillinger about the hard ice of the bay, and Mr.

Dillinger had just shaken his head and gone to work. Now the skates were back the way Travis liked them, even at his most fussy.

He hadn't cut any corners. He had his lucky underwear on. He had tied his right skate first, and then his left. He had wrapped his ankles in shinpad tape. He had kissed the inside of his sweater as he yanked it over his head. He had placed his hand on the "C" stitched over his heart. "C" for captain.

But it still wasn't right. He had only one stick. He liked to have two, minimum, each one as new as possible. Each with the same curve – a "Russian curve," he called it, with a slight flick at the end – and each freshly taped with black tape on the blade and white tape on the handle. Muck had taught him that. "Black tape will rot out the palms of your gloves," he had said, "white tape won't."

But *one* stick – he had only *one* stick. He had brought three up, all brand-new. One he'd given to the captain of the Mighty Geese, the first team they had played. The other he had taken to the camp and stupidly left there. Now he was down to one stick, and if something happened to that one, then he didn't know what he would do.

Muck seemed happy. He had no plays to go over, no hockey to discuss, but he did insist on making a speech.

"This is the icing on the cake," he told them.

"You kids have had one of the greatest experiences of your lives up here, and you should be thinking about that when you're out there on the ice.

"We're playing our hosts. If not for them, you wouldn't be here. That doesn't mean you give them the victory – a win that comes that way is really a defeat – but it does mean you play with courtesy. No cheap stuff. No showing off. Listening, Nishikawa? Nothing but a mature approach and good hockey. Understand?"

No one said a word. No one ever had to say a word after Muck had spoken.

Travis was captain. He knew his job. This was his cue. He leapt to his feet.

"*Let's go, Screech Owls!*"

Nish jumped up after him.

"*Screech Owls, Screech Owls . . . GO, SCREECH OWLS!*"

16

THE ATMOSPHERE AT THE WASKAGANISH COMMUNITY Arena was electric. The little rink was packed so tight, there wasn't an empty seat to be found. The entire village was there. And all the other teams. It felt like Hockey Night in Canada, not Hockey Night in Waskaganish. He could hear the cheers, the boos, the thundering clap of the public address system as the Wolverines' came onto the ice.

> *We will,*
> *We will,*
> *ROCK YOU!*

Travis rounded the net and did his sweet little hop. He skipped slightly, shrugging his shoulders. He felt good. But he couldn't help thinking about his missing stick. What if he broke his last one?

The Owls warmed up Chantal, who was getting the start on the basis of her play in the game Travis and Nish and Jesse had missed. Travis hit the crossbar – the good luck sign he needed.

The warm-up over, the Screech Owls gathered at the net to charge themselves up. They rapped Chantal's pads. They tapped each other's shins. Travis knocked helmets with Chantal, then his linemates, Dmitri and Derek, then Nish. He usually stopped there, but he found himself going to Jesse and tapping him, helmet to helmet. Travis led the team cheer: "*Screech Owls, Screech Owls . . . GO, SCREECH OWLS!*"

Travis skated out to take the face-off. He looked into the stands and saw Chief Ottereyes sitting with Jesse and Rachel's grandparents. They had come in from the camp to see the game.

He scanned the crowd and found his parents, waving to him. He saw where the Moose Factory Mighty Geese were all sitting.

Travis was facing off against Jimmy Whiskey-jack, his host and the Wolverines' captain. Jimmy winked and tapped Travis's pads with his stick. Travis returned the tap. The big, surly assistant captain was on defence, already scowling at him. Rachel wasn't on the ice. He checked the Wolverines' bench. She was sitting, waiting. He could see the "A" on her sweater.

When the puck dropped, he wasn't paying full attention. The Wolverines' captain swept it away easily, sending it back to the big defenceman. Travis and Dmitri both gave chase (Muck usually wanted only one to forecheck), and the defence-man waited until the last possible second before flipping the puck up to the left winger. Travis and Dmitri turned into each other, catching up in each other's sticks and legs. Travis went down.

The winger hit Jimmy Whiskeyjack as he made the blueline. The Wolverines' captain deftly flipped the puck over Data's stick and then was all alone, bearing down on Chantal.

Until Nish hit him. Nish simply threw his body at Jimmy, cutting him off and knocking the puck off the stick before, spinning like a top, he tore the legs out from under him. The puck dribbled away harmlessly into the pads of Chantal, who covered up.

"*Alrriigght, Nish!*" Travis shouted. Good old Nish – he had saved the day.

They lined up for the face-off. The big defenceman moved up tight, hoping for a quick shot. Nish took note and shifted.

"*Hey, Moose Nostrils!*" the big defenceman called.

"*Whadya say, Bear Butt?*" Nish called back.

Travis laughed. He knew Nish was here to play. It was going to be a game.

Travis won this face-off. He dropped it back to Nish, who circled his net and hit Dmitri along the boards by the hash marks. Dmitri chopped the puck out into centre, where Derek picked it up and headed for the blueline, the big defenceman backpedalling at full speed.

Derek carried the puck over the line, then left it there while he and the defenceman came together in what looked like, but certainly was not, an accidental collision. The puck sat waiting for Travis, who scooped it up, danced past the defenceman, and put a nifty pass over to Dmitri, who one-timed it off the crossbar.

"OHHH NO!" Travis shouted.

Back on the bench, Muck patted their shoulders. He liked what he was seeing, even though they had no goal to show for it. Travis couldn't stop his legs from jumping with nervous energy. He sat, anxious to get right back out.

Liz's line was on now against Rachel Highboy's. Rachel had the speed, and she also had a big centre with good reach. The centre beat Andy Higgins to a puck and swept it away. Wilson missed it and Rachel flew past him, picking it up and moving in, one-on-one, on Chantal. Rachel deked once and went to her backhand, and roofed a beauty as she pulled around the net.

Wolverines 1, Screech Owls 0.

They flooded the ice between periods. Just like the NHL. Floods, stop time, announcements, goal judges. In the dressing room, Muck seemed content with the way things were going, even though the Owls had failed to score and were now behind in the game.

"Just keep doing what you're doing," Muck said. "It'll come."

He walked to the centre of the room and paused. "Nishikawa," he said.

Nish, who had been bending down, catching his breath, looked up, wincing.

Muck almost smiled. "That's hockey you're playing, son."

Travis knew what he meant. Nish was playing the game of his life. He was being double-shifted by Muck and never seemed to stop moving out there. No stupid rushes, no foolish pinches, just Nish at his best: steady, dependable, good on the rush and absolutely perfect on defence.

"You're playing great, man," Travis said as they walked down the corridor to start the next period.

"I have to."

Nish said nothing more. He moved ahead of Travis when they hit the ice, sticking to himself.

Travis's line was starting again. He won this face-off and got the puck back to Nish, who kept it long enough to draw his check. Nish then flipped the puck back to Travis, who headed down-ice, slowly looping when he made the blueline so he could see where Dmitri and Derek were going to be.

Travis hadn't even been looking at his stick or the puck when the big defenceman slashed him. All he felt was the jolt.

The whistle blew. And then, when he looked down, he saw his stick was broken. He threw down what was left of it. Good, at least the big guy was going to get a penalty.

"*Number 7!*" the referee shouted. "*Let's go!*"

Number 7? Travis turned and looked at the defenceman, now skating away. He was wearing number 22. Number 7 was Travis Lindsay.

The referee was glaring at him and pointing to the penalty box. "*Let's go!*"

Travis couldn't believe his ears. "What for?"

"Two minutes for playing with a broken stick! Now let's go! Or it's two minutes more for unsportsmanlike conduct!"

Travis couldn't believe it, but he knew better than to argue. He skated to the penalty box, where the door was already swinging open.

He could hear the cheers. He could hear the odd boo from the Screech Owls' supporters, but it wasn't very loud or very serious. Everyone knew Travis had made a mistake.

Derek skated across with a new stick. He handed it over the boards to Travis.

"You haven't got any left," Derek said. "This one's Liz's. They're almost the same."

Travis took it. They *were* almost the same, but there was still a world of difference. He felt the stick. A left lie, but Liz never put a Russian curve in hers. Neither did she tape the handle the same way. He stood in the penalty box and flexed it, but it didn't feel at all right.

The Owls were shorthanded now with Travis in the penalty box, although it didn't seem that way. The Wolverines were a good team – they moved the puck well, and they shot well from the point, particularly the big defenceman who'd broken Travis's stick – but Travis couldn't believe the way Nish was playing. He was diving in front of pucks. He was ragging the puck and breaking up rushes, and once he even took the puck up-ice and had an excellent shot himself, only to have it tick off the post. When Nish went to the bench at the end of his shift, every fan in the building rose in tribute to him. Nish never even looked up. He sat on the bench, his head down between his legs, gasping for air. From the penalty box on the far side of the rink, Travis could see Muck lay a hand on Nish's neck as he passed behind him. He knew Nish would feel it. He knew Nish would know whose hand it was and what it meant.

"*Hey, Travis!*"

Travis turned, not recognizing the voice.

The captain of the Moose Factory Mighty Geese was standing behind him. He was holding up Travis's stick, the one Travis had given him.

"Looks like you need this back, pal."

Travis took it, flexed it on the floor of the penalty box. It felt great! Perfect! He looked back at his new friend and smiled.

"Thanks," he said.

"Get a goal for me," said the captain of the Mighty Geese.

17

TWO WOLVERINES, THE CAPTAIN AND THE BIG defenceman, came down, two-on-one, on Nish. Nish waited, then lunged, brilliantly poking the puck free and up to Derek. Derek turned immediately and hit Travis, who was circling just outside the blueline. The puck felt right on his blade. It was good to have his old stick back.

Travis hit Dmitri right at the opposition blueline. Dmitri swept past the one remaining defenceman and shot, the slapper catching the Wolverines' goaltender on the chest and bouncing back out toward the blueline, where Nish cradled it in his glove and dropped it onto the blade of his stick.

Nish pivoted beautifully, hit Jesse Highboy, coming on in a quick change, with a beautifully feathered pass, and Jesse rifled a shot high in under the crossbar.

Wolverines 1, Screech Owls 1.

The crowd went wild. A goal by the visitors, yes, but a goal by a *Highboy*. They stood and cheered, and cheered again when the announcement was made. Travis skated back to the bench, where Nish was already sitting, trying to catch his breath.

"Great poke check," Travis told him.

Nish looked up, grinning. "An old man taught it to me."

At the next intermission, Muck had nothing to say. He seemed satisfied. Travis had already spoken to him in the corridor, and now Muck stood in the middle of the room and signalled to Travis that it was time for him to speak.

"Your captain has something to say," Muck said.

Travis stood up and cleared his throat.

"We've had a great time here," he said, "no matter whether we win or lose. You all saw that first team we played. No equipment. No gloves. Players had to share equipment. What do you say we leave behind some stuff for them?"

No one said anything. Perhaps they weren't listening. But then Nish began to tap his stick on the cement floor, and soon everyone was tapping their sticks. The answer was yes.

The Screech Owls then played what they would later call their best period ever.

They couldn't get by the big defenceman, and they couldn't get the puck past the Wolverines' goaltender, but it was the same for the opposition. They attacked, especially Jimmy Whiskey-jack and the big defenceman and Rachel, but they couldn't get past Nish. He seemed to be everywhere. Travis looked at his friend and knew that he had found his "zone." He was playing a game that should have been impossible. And if he had wanted to prove a point, he was proving it. No one was calling him Moose Nostrils any more.

Nish broke up another play and sent Dmitri away with the puck. One of the defencemen had been caught pinching in, and the other fell when Dmitri's startling speed caught him off guard. The only Wolverine to make it back was the assistant captain, Rachel Highboy. Dmitri tried to take her off into the corner, but she wouldn't go for the move, so he looped at the blueline and hit Travis coming in.

It was perfect. If Nish had found his "zone," then Travis had found his, too. Everything felt absolutely right: the skates like part of his feet, the stick like an extension of his arms. *He would try his new play!*

He came as close to Rachel as he dared, and then, just as she was about to poke out, he dropped the puck back into his skates. It hit the left one perfectly. The puck bounced with his stride, heading for the right skate – but it never arrived!

He dug in, falling as he turned. Rachel Highboy, with the puck, was moving fast up the ice. She hit Jimmy Whiskeyjack at the blueline, and Jimmy fed it back to her along the boards. She put a pass back, and he one-timed the shot, the puck just clearing a falling, desperate Nish and passing under the blocker arm of Chantal.

Wolverines 2, Screech Owls 1.

In the dying minutes, Nish gave everything he had. He rushed the puck. He shot. He set up plays. He broke up plays. After Muck pulled Chantal for an extra attacker in the final minute, he even stopped a couple of sure goals. But he couldn't do enough.

The Screech Owls had lost.

The horn blew, and the place went wild. It wasn't just the cheering, which was deafening – standing and cheering was not enough. The stands emptied! The crowd poured onto the ice and lifted Rachel and Jimmy Whiskeyjack and the big defenceman and the goaltender onto their shoulders. They sang and cheered and the loudspeakers rumbled with the Wolverines' theme song.

We will,
We will,
ROCK YOU!

Travis couldn't feel bad. The Owls had played well. He had made a mistake, but, as Muck often said, "Hockey is a game of mistakes." And Rachel

Highboy had turned his dumb play to her advantage. The hometown team had won, and Travis knew how much that meant.

They lined up to shake hands. Travis congratulated everyone, and when he came to Rachel, she laughed and smiled.

"You shouldn't have showed me that move on the bay," she said.

Travis felt foolish. "I guess not."

She smiled again. "You're a wonderful player."

And then she was gone. Travis hurried through the line, feeling as if he'd just won the Stanley Cup. He had never felt so fantastic in his life!

They lined up at the bluelines. Chief Ottereyes said a few words into a microphone that were lost completely in the echo, but no one was much interested in speeches anyway.

Then the Chief announced the Most Valuable Players from each team. Now everyone paid attention, and when it turned out to be the cousins, Rachel and Jesse Highboy, both sides cheered.

They gave Jesse a new hockey stick, and he immediately skated over to the boards where his family was sitting and handed it to his grandfather, who took it with a smile. The people cheered. But maybe only Travis knew what Jesse meant by giving his prize to his grandfather. He had taught Jesse the secrets of the bush that had saved them. And he had found them in the wilderness. What would have happened if he hadn't come along? Besides, Jesse's grandfather needed a stick. He couldn't go on playing forever with a shovel.

The Chief then announced that there was also a prize for the defensive player of the game. Both sides went quiet so they could hear, but there was never any doubt who would win it.

"Wayne Nishikawa," Chief Ottereyes announced.

Everyone cheered. Both teams slammed their sticks on the ice in appreciation. Nish skated out, saluting the crowd, and took his prize from the Chief.

It was an Ojibway dream catcher.

When Rachel Highboy saw, she yelled, "*From what I've seen, you could really use one!*"

"*Moose Nostrils thanks you!*" he called back. She laughed, along with several other Wolverines who heard him over the din.

●

Back in the dressing room, Muck shook everyone's hand. He did this only on rare occasions, and this was indeed a rare occasion. No one talked about losing. No one felt as if they had lost.

"This pile in the centre," Travis announced, tossing down his stick. "This is what we give to the Mighty Geese."

One by one, the Screech Owls tossed in their sticks. Barry, the assistant coach, grabbed the entire rack of extras and dumped them into the growing pile in the centre of the room.

"They need gloves, too," said Nish, and tossed his in.

Travis couldn't believe it. What would Nish's parents say? He decided his friend had the right idea, though, and pulled his own gloves off and tossed them onto the pile. Several others followed suit.

Mr. Dillinger walked over with a handful of the skates he carried in the equipment box for emergencies and dumped them all down without a word.

Nish then threw his own skates in, the ice still glistening on the blades.

Not bad, Travis thought, for a guy who wanted to leave the second he got here.

18

TRAVIS DIDN'T WANT IT TO COME TO AN END. BUT it was time to go. The sun was out, the sky as blue as the Maple Leafs' away jerseys, and the entire village had once again come out to the airstrip – on snowmobiles, in pick-ups, and by foot – to see the Screech Owls. Only this time the Owls were going home.

There were actually more people there to see them off than had seen them arrive. The Moose Factory Mighty Geese were out in force. The captain had brought Travis's stick to get it autographed by all the Owls.

"We're going to keep this as our good-luck stick," the captain said.

"Then you should have taken one of mine," Nish said.

No one had changed as much as Nish. He was friendly now. He and the Wolverines' big defenceman had struck up a friendship at the final-night banquet – where the menu had featured burgers and fries and pizza – and Nish had even promised to come up and visit again. Even more startling, they had brought in some moose nostrils, and, to great cheering, Nish had had his photograph taken eating some.

"I guess I won't see you for a while."

It was Rachel. She was alone, smiling, but she did not look happy.

"We're already talking about inviting the Wolverines down for a return match," said Travis.

"That would be nice."

They stood staring at each other for a few seconds. It struck Travis that he might not see her again.

"I'll send you whatever Mr. Dillinger writes up for the paper," he said.

"Thanks."

Travis cleared his throat. He didn't know what to say.

"I really like that dream catcher," he said.

"Use it," Rachel said. "It's specially for you."

"Yeah, well . . . see you."

Rachel said nothing. She reached out and touched his lips with the tip of her mitten – then she was gone.

"ALLL ABBBOARRRDD!" Mr. Dillinger called out.

They began climbing the steps to the Dash 8. Travis turned just before the door and looked back. Rachel was standing at the back of the crowd, on a snowbank, alone. She waved.

Travis turned back and bumped into Nish, who had also stopped at the door to look back.

"She waved at me," Nish said.

Travis started to open his mouth to correct him when Nish gave him a big wink. Chuckling to himself, Nish moved ahead down the aisle and found a seat. Travis joined him. Still laughing to himself, Nish bent down and began removing goodies from his pack: bannock, and wild meat. Travis could see the MVP award, the dream catcher, carefully placed in Nish's pack.

Out over the water, the plane hit the first turbulence. It bucked, settled, then bucked again wildly as the pilot tried to rise into smoother air. But all he found was more pockets as the north wind struck the shore of James Bay and rose right over the village. The plane bucked, fell, jacked sideways, and bucked again.

"I'M GONNA HURL!"

THE END

Murder at Hockey Camp

Travis, Nish, and the rest of the Screech Owls are in the heart of cottage country to spend a week at summer hockey camp. Joining them for some off-season practice is Sarah Cuthbertson – the Owls' former captain – with her new team, the Junior Aeros. It promises to be a wonderful seven days of sun, sand, and skating. Nish is even planning the World's Biggest Skinny Dip!

But it's not all fun and sun. The owner of the camp, Buddy O'Reilly, is a tyrant – a surly former NHLer, even meaner now than he was as a player. Soon coach Muck Munro, who never believed in summer hockey in the first place, has to warn the bully to stay away from the Screech Owls.

Next morning dawns bright and warm – but not warm enough to stir the cold body hidden in the boathouse! Now a killer is at large, and the Screech Owls are right in the middle of a real-life murder case.

Chapter 1

TRAVIS LINDSAY SHUDDERED. HE COULDN'T HELP himself. He had never seen – or felt – anything quite so frightening, so powerful, so absolutely raw.

The storm had broken over the lake. The boys in cabin 4 – which was known as "Osprey" – had seen it coming all afternoon: big bruised fists of cloud heading straight for the camp, the sky dark as night even before the dinner-bell rang. They had gathered on the steps of the cabin to listen to the growling and rumbling as the storm approached, and watch the far shore flicker from time to time under distant lightning.

There was a flash, and Nish began counting off the distance: "One steamboat . . . two steamboat . . . three steamboat . . . four steamboat . . ." A clap of thunder cut him off, the sound growing as it reached them. "Four miles," Nish announced matter-of-factly. Nish the expert. Nish the Great Outdoorsman ever since the Screech Owls' trip up North, when he nearly froze to death because of his own stupidity.

Then came the first overhead burst, and not even Nish dared speak. Directly above them, the sky simply split. It broke apart and emptied, the rain instantly thick and hard as water from a fire hose. The boys scrambled for the safety of the cabin and the comforting slam of the screen door. Travis had his hands over his ears, but it was useless. The second crack, even closer, was like a cannon going off beside them. The air sizzled as if the thunder clap had caused the rain to boil, and the walls of the little cabin bounced in the sudden, brilliant flashes of light that accompanied the explosion.

Not even a half steamboat, Nish, Travis thought to himself. Not even a *row*boat between flash and thunder. The storm was right on top of them!

The six boys in "Osprey" moved to the window. Wayne Nishikawa in front, then Gordie Griffith, Larry "Data" Ulmar, Andy Higgins, Lars "Cherry" Johanssen, and, behind them all, Travis Lindsay, the Screech Owls' captain. They could barely see in the sudden dark of the storm, but then lightning flashed again, and instantly their world was as bright as if a strobe light had gone off. The streak of lightning seemed to freeze momentarily, like a great fiery crack in the dark windshield of the sky. Again they heard the sizzle of fire. And again thunder struck immediately, the walls bouncing, Travis shaking. He felt cold and frightened.

Another flash, and they could see, perfectly, as if in a painting, the girls' camp across the water. Travis wondered if Sarah was watching. Sarah Cuthbertson had been captain of the Owls before Travis, and her new team, the Toronto

Junior Aeros, were in six cabins out on the nearest island, along with the three girls – Jennie, Liz, and Chantal – who played for the Owls.

In the long weeks leading up to the end of the school year and the start of summer hockey camp, Travis thought he had anticipated every part of the upcoming adventure. Swimming . . . swinging off the rope into the lake . . . diving from the cliffs . . . waterskiing and fishing and campfires . . . even the mosquitoes. But he hadn't imagined anything like this.

The storm held over them, the explosions now coming so fast it was impossible to tell which clap of thunder belonged to which flash of lightning. It seemed the world was ending. The light over the lake flickered like a lamp with a short circuit. The rain pounded on the roof. The door rattled in the wind. And Travis shook as if he were standing naked outdoors in winter instead of indoors, in a track suit, in July.

It wasn't the cold so much as the feeling of helplessness, the insignificance. Being afraid of the dark was nothing compared to this. He'd gladly trade this unearthly light for pitch black and a thousand snakes and rats and black widow spiders and slimy one-eyed monsters lurking at the foot of his bed back home, where there had never, ever, been a storm like this one . . .

KKKKKKRRRRRAAAAACKKKKKKKKK!!

They saw a flash and heard a snap of thunder

– but the sound that followed was new! It was a cracking, followed by a rushing sound, then a crash that made the cabin jump and the boys fall, screaming, to their knees.

"*What the hell?*" shouted Nish.

"*The roof blew off!*" yelled Data.

But it wasn't the roof! They were still dry! Andy Higgins, who was the tallest, was the first to stretch up and look out to see what had happened.

"Look at that!"

Now they were all up to see.

"What happened?"

"Lemme see!"

Travis looked out through the rain-dimpled window. One pane of glass was broken, and wind and water were coming in on their faces. Outside, the lawn had vanished. Across the grass, lying right between their cabin and "Loon," the next cabin over – where Willie Granger and Wilson Kelly and Fahd Noorizadeh and Jesse Highboy were staying – was a huge, shattered hemlock, its trunk split and its wood as white as skin where the bark had been ripped away.

It had missed both cabins by a matter of inches.

Travis began to shake even harder.

Kidnapped in Sweden

The Screech Owls are off to Stockholm to take part in the first-ever International Goodwill Pee Wee Tournament, featuring teams from Finland, Norway, the Czech Republic, Germany, and Russia, as well as from all over Sweden.

Not only do the Owls get to go on the trip of a lifetime, they also learn the differences between European and North American hockey and make some great new friends – including the thirteen-year-old Russian phenomenon Slava Shadrin, who is already being called "the next Pavel Bure."

The young hockey star even travels with his own bodyguards. The police, it turns out, suspect the "Russian Mob" is planning to kidnap Slava and hold him for ransom!

And sure enough, when Slava and his new Screech Owls friends give his bodyguards the slip, the Mob moves in. But the villains end up with more captives than they intended . . .

Terror in Florida

When Travis, Nish, Sarah, and the rest of the gang pile onto a school bus headed for Florida, the Screech Owls expect a spring break filled with sun, sand, and lots of ice. With luck they may even make it to the peewee tournament final, to be held in the magnificent Ice Palace, home of the NHL's Tampa Bay Lightning!

Muck and Mr. Dillinger have planned a fun trip. As well as camping and swimming, they'll get to go to Disney World. Nish, of course, has bigger ideas. With his new X-ray glasses he bought on the "stupid stop" on the way down, he's hoping to see a lot more than just tourist attractions.

The only trouble is, Nish ends up seeing too much! Travis wasn't looking forward to riding the Tower of Terror at the Disney-MGM Studios, but it's going to take even more courage to face this. The Screech Owls have uncovered a plot to terrorize all of America!

THE SEVENTH BOOK IN THE SCREECH OWLS SERIES

The Quebec City Crisis

It is Winter Carnival time in beautiful Quebec City. The Screech Owls are in town to join in the winter fun and take part in the biggest hockey tournament on Earth: the famous Quebec Peewee Invitational. This is where Guy Lafleur, Wayne Gretzky, and Mario Lemieux first showed the world their incredible talents – and now it's the turn of Travis, Nish, Sarah, and their friends.

But the dream trip soon turns into a nightmare. Travis is asked to keep a diary that will be published in one of the big daily newspapers – and a terrible misunderstanding follows. Soon after Travis's words appear in print, the crowds are booing the Screech Owls, and someone – no one knows who – begins a reign of terror against the team.

The Owls know they are good enough to make it to the final. Sarah could even equal the tournament record set by the great Guy Lafleur! But if the Owls are to stand any chance at all, they must first find out who is trying to destroy them.

THE SCREECH OWLS SERIES

Also available in five omnibus editions!